Who Wants Forever
An Emerald Isle Enchantment Novel

By

Dena Garson

WHO WANTS FOREVER
Copyright © 2019 Dena Garson
Edited by Heather Long

Cover design by Cover Couture
www.bookcovercouture.com
Photo Copyright: Kanuman / Shutterstock
Photo Copyright: ArtofPhotos / Shutterstock
Photo Copyright: Rob Stark / Shutterstock

All rights reserved.

ISBN (print): 978-1-945075-13-1

DEDICATION

For my boys – always and forever.

 1

"REAGHAN, daughter of Owin, bobbled her curtsey when the sprouts growing in crystal bowls lining the long tables to her left snagged her interest.

"I saw that, you know." Caoilfhinn, Reaghan's cousin and newly crowned fae queen, teased.

"Of course you did, my queen." Reaghan's grin expanded. "It's just one of your many gifts."

Caoilfhinn arched a single brow. "Did you come to help with my seedlings or to mock your queen?"

"I would never mock my queen." Reaghan's lip twitched with mirth. "But I will always tease my cousin."

"Hmmmm." Caoilfhinn pointed at a tray of tiny plants. "How about if you make yourself helpful and bring those."

"I live but to serve you, my queen." Reaghan grinned without repentance.

"Oh just stop it." Caoilfhinn rolled her eyes and motioned for Reaghan to follow. "You know I'm not used to having people bow and cater to me."

"I know. I'll go easy on you. For a while."

"Gee, thanks." Caoilfhinn stopped next to the area cleared of old plants, then knelt. She gestured for Reaghan to sit nearby. "How are things with Pryderi?"

"Fine." Reaghan admired the variety of blooming shrubs and flowers around them. It was one of her favorite places in all of Eolande. Some of the realm's most beautiful plants could be found in the queen's garden.

Caoilfhinn crinkled her nose. "That doesn't sound exciting at all."

Reaghan snorted. "That would be an accurate description."

A hand tool appeared and dug several small holes near the edge of the pathway when Caoilfhinn waved her hand. "Have you accepted the marriage contract yet?"

"No."

Instead of using her powers, Caoilfhinn motioned for Reaghan to hand her one of the plants from the tray. "Are you going to?"

"Do I really have a choice?"

Caoilfhinn stopped what she was doing. "Yes, you do."

"Then why does it feel like I don't?"

"Because, as usual, the men involved in the agreement think they know best." Caoilfhinn situated the tiny sprout the way she wanted and filled the hole in around it. "Do you care for Pryderi?"

Reaghan didn't even have to search her heart to know the answer. She had debated the issue more times than she cared to admit. "As a friend, yes."

"But not as a lover?"

"No. It has never been that way between us."

"Are you certain?"

"Quite." Reaghan handed Caoilfhinn another sprout. "Several seasons ago, when we were both between attachments, we tried to see if anything sparked." Her cheeks grew warm but she shrugged it off. "All we succeeded in doing was embarrassing ourselves and proving what we both already knew."

"What did you know?"

"That we're better off remaining just friends."

Another sprout went into a hole. "How does he feel about the agreement?"

"The same as me. That it's easier to keep pretending that we're waiting for the right time to announce something." Reaghan was certainly in no hurry to endure that conversation. To say her mother and father were not going to be pleased would be an understatement.

"Are you certain of his feelings?"

"I am."

"I thought I had noticed the faint sparkle of a love bond the last time I saw him."

"You probably did."

Caoilfhinn frowned then her gaze became distant. "He loves another."

Reaghan smiled sadly. "Yes." Learning he loved someone else had been a disappointment at first. But after some intense soul searching she realized her feelings of loss were due more to the fact she had yet to find someone to love and be loved by.

Caoilfhinn blinked away the vision. "You knew this."

"I did."

"Tell me."

"You already know, do you not?" Since Caoilfhinn became Queen her powers had vastly expanded. Most especially those pertaining to prophecy.

"I want to hear it from your perspective."

Reaghan handed Caoilfhinn another plant. "Her name is Kaasi. As you probably already know, she's the daughter of Genaine."

Caoilfhinn grimaced. "Their families will never approve the match."

"No. They will not. And Pryderi has no delusions otherwise." Rivalries and politics between the fae aristocrats were not for the faint of heart. As the daughter of one of the first royal families, there was no escaping it.

Caoilfhinn dug six more holes. "So he pretends to consider the marriage agreement with you while secretly seeing Kaasi."

"That is correct."

"And you're okay with that?"

Reaghan shrugged. "It was my idea." She smiled when Caoilfhinn's head snapped up. It wasn't often she managed to surprise her cousin.

"After I was attacked by the vampire, mother did everything in her power to keep me at home. To the point that it interfered with my training and they threatened to dismiss me. We argued every time I returned to my classes. Father agreed to support me and my training if I agreed to consider the marriage contract with Pryderi."

Caoilfhinn shook her head as she filled in another hole.

"It didn't take long for me to realize the primary benefit of being in a pre-contract relationship."

"And what benefits would you be referring to? You've already said sex between you Pryderi is off the table."

A snort escaped before Reaghan could stifle it. "The string of marriage hungry suitors virtually disappeared. It left me in a unique position to evaluate potential suitors without external pressure."

"Ah." Caoilfhinn nodded as she sprinkled pale purple foam over the plants she had been working with. Almost instantly each one perked up and produced a tiny blue bud. "And what did you discover during your covert search?"

"Mostly that what I want, what I believe in my heart to be what I need in order to truly be happy, may not exist."

"You're still young. There is still time for you to find what you want and need."

Reaghan hung her head. "At this point I have met all of the eligible bachelors here in Eolande. Between my training and my personal travels, I have been to almost every human country." She shrugged. "My visits to the mortal plane spanned multiple generations. Yet not once have I made a connection with anyone that I felt would last a lifetime. Much less a fae lifetime."

Caoilfhinn wiped the dirt from her fingers then reached for one of Reaghan's hands. "The lore doesn't lie. There is someone for everyone. Our other half, if you will. The trick is being patient until you find them." The queen's eyes swirled with the misty gray fog that indicated she was peering into the beyond. "You will find yours when the time is right and not a minute before. That time is drawing near though."

Reaghan waited silently for fear that she might interrupt the vision's flow and miss some key piece of information about the man meant for her.

"He will be strong. A leader. The sound of his voice holds the power to sway even the hardest of hearts. But darkness surrounds him." Caoilfhinn sucked in a breath of air and squeezed Reaghan's hand.

The mention of darkness sent chills down Reaghan's back.

"The darkness grips him tightly. He feels as if he has been consumed by it. That his very soul is scarred. But you will bring light to his life. Light that has been missing for more than a century."

Reaghan's heart skipped a beat. A century. Not a human then.

Her cousin shook off the effects of her vision. She patted Reaghan's hand and smiled. "Remind me again. What human name do you usually use?"

"Reaghan McCarthy."

Caoilfhinn nodded. "A good name."

"Your Majesty." One of Caoilfhinn's attendants called out as she rushed toward them, preventing Reaghan from asking any questions. When the attendant reached them, she dropped into a curtsy. "Councilman Sativola has sent a message." She handed a folded parchment to the queen.

Caoilfhinn took the missive and scanned its contents. She was frowning by the time she reached the end. "Thank you, Locklyn. That will be all."

"Yes, my queen." Locklyn bobbed a courtesy then hurried away.

Whatever Caoilfhinn had read obviously bothered her a great deal. She stabbed the hand-tool she had been using into the ground then stared at the new plants with a frown.

"Everything all right?" Reaghan finally asked.

"We don't have much time."

Her entire body tensed. "For what?"

"I need a favor of you."

"Of course." She lifted her chin. "I'd be happy to help you with anything you need."

Setting the tool she had been using aside, Caoilfhinn motioned to Reaghan. "Come with me. I don't want to risk being overheard."

Curious what the queen might tell her that would be so secret, Reaghan followed. Caoilfhinn led her to center of the garden. They stopped near a large stone fountain that bubbled and gushed sparkling streams of purple and blue liquid over pale white stone.

"I'm sure you have heard about the daughter of Sativola."

Reaghan nodded. "Yes, of course. She's the girl who went missing in the mortal plane not long ago." It was a shocking story. She prayed Eirin was simply being reckless and ignoring her parents' attempts to contact her.

Caoilfhinn grimaced. "There are few who haven't heard about it at this point."

"People do talk."

"Yes, they do. And often, too much.

The favor I need relates to the council sessions about her."

"The council." Reaghan frowned. Doubt crept in diminishing the excitement she originally experienced at being asked to help her queen. "Are you certain you would not be better off talking with Father?"

"No, I most certainly would not. What I need neither your father nor your brother can provide. And I trust no one else to accomplish the task."

Reaghan's chest swelled with pride. "What would you have me do?"

"I want you to go to the mortal plane and ascertain the status and mindset of Eirin, Daughter of Sativola."

"Her mindset?"

"Yes." Caoilfhinn gestured for Reaghan to sit on the edge of the fountain with her. "I need to know whether or not she is being held in thrall or against her will."

"Who would be holding her against her will? Eirin may be young, but she isn't without skill. And in the mortal plane, she should be more than capable of overpowering any mortal."

"Her father believes she has come under the influence of a vampire."

Reaghan stiffened as flashes of the vampire attack she'd suffered bubbled up through her memories. She quickly shut them off and focused on what Caoilfhinn was saying.

"I am aware of your own experience with the human undead. And while it seems cruel to expose you to something you have every reason to hate, I am afraid that I have no other choice." Caoilfhinn dipped her fingers into the fountain. The flow of lavender liquid immediately reversed itself.

"The council is at odds. Lairgnen and I are being pressed for a decision on the matter. I do not believe, however, that we have been given all of the facts. Worse, I believe some of the information we have been given is, shall we say, inaccurate." Caoilfhinn shrugged. "At a minimum, skewed in a manner that suits one side or the other. If this matter cannot be cleared soon, we may find ourselves at war."

Reaghan's hands clenched into fists. Fear warred with anger. Why were some people in such a hurry to start wars? Yes, she had been trained to fight. Because of her history, she wanted to be able to defend herself. It didn't mean she wanted to use those skills on everyone she met. "Surely there is something that can be done to prevent war."

"There is." Caoilfhinn captured her gaze." My solution however requires your help."

"How?"

"Find Eirin."

"And when I do?"

"If she is being held against her will or under nefarious circumstances, free her. If she remains in the mortal plan of her own free will, I need her confession."

Tamping down old fears, Reaghan focused on her task. "What of the vampire?"

"If he possesses a threat to you or to her, do what you must."

"Very well." Reaghan wiped her palm against her thigh. "How will I get through the portal?"

"I will open one."

"Won't the elders sense it?"

Caoilfhinn shook her head. "Not if it isn't open long." A noise near the entry caught their attention. In a lower voice, Caoilfhinn rushed to add, "Meet me here in the garden after first supper. Tell no one. Carry only what you must. I'll supply you with enough coin to purchase whatever you need in the mortal world."

"How shall I return?"

"I'll reopen the same gate in three human days."

Reaghan's brows rose in surprise.

"I am afraid that is all the time I can give you to find Eirin. Any longer and I fear we will have to take steps that none of us are prepared for."

"What should I tell Mother and Father?"

"Nothing." Caoilfhinn waved her hand in the air. "Leave that to me."

"Very well." It was a relief to know she wouldn't have to deal with her mother's reaction.

Caoilfhinn quickly added, "The vampire they believe has taken Eirin is expected to attend the vampire clan meeting at Tullamore Castle. That meeting is your best chance of finding Eirin or at least obtaining enough information to find her."

An entire clan of vampires? Could she really do this? It didn't look as if there was another option. "When will that meeting be held?"

"It's a three day event that begins tonight." Caoilfhinn raised one finger. "And I have an idea for getting you into the hotel where the meeting is being held."

"I don't have to be a building inspector or something equally tedious, do I? You know I don't mind learning new human oddities, but some of those jobs are horribly dull to read about." She clung to humor to drown out the fear threatening to bubble to the surface.

The narrow braids that hung near Caoilfhinn temple swayed as she shook her head. "No. Nothing like that. But you will need your violin."

Reaghan's brow rose with curiosity.

"There is one thing you should know since you have never been there. Tullamore grounds are considered neutral territory. There is absolutely no fighting allowed. And your glamour, no matter how good it is, will not fool the castle care takers. I think it best if you do not reveal your true self to any mortals, vampires, or any Others you come in contact with." Concern flickered across Caoilfhinn's normally impassive expression. "No sense in riling any of the clans unnecessarily."

"I understand." Ideas floated through her mind of the things she would need to take with her.

"And Reaghan, you must return home before sunrise on the fourth day. If you remain in the mortal world for even one moment past sunrise the portal will be closed to you and I may not able to open it again for some time." She reached for Reaghan's hand. "You do understand how important it is that we obtain an accurate accounting of Eirin's state of mind, do you not?"

"I do understand." Reaghan lifted her chin. "I swear I will do everything in my power to find Eirin and learn what has become of her."

"Good." Caoilfhinn got to her feet. "Now go. We both have things to do to prepare."

"I will see you tonight." Reaghan made her courtesy and turned to go.

"And Reaghan?" She waited until Reaghan faced her again. "Thank you."

"You're welcome, cousin." With one last dip of her head she hurried away from the queen's garden.

 2

AMARANDE Maniaci looked out at the Tullamore grounds from the window of his sire's suite as he waited for his clan patriarch to finish his call. Gas lamps lining the garden paths below flickered and the branches of nearby trees swayed as the wind picked up.

"My apologies, Amarande."

Amarande turned when he heard his name. Edrigu Moreschi smiled fondly and moved forward with his arms outstretched. Amarande gladly returned his patriarch's embrace. It had been far too long since they had seen each other. And even longer since he had been home. He missed his family and his clan more than he had allowed himself to think about.

"I trust your trip went well?" Edrigu asked when he released Amarande.

"It did. Nerea's arrangements were exceptional as always. Please give her my thanks."

"Glad to hear it. Have you had any word from Valter?"

"No, not yet. I sent a courtesy message to let him know I arrived."

"I do not like this upstart pack leader." Edrigu practically spat Valter's title. "His dealings so far have been rash and bordering on insult. I want to know immediately if he or any of his pack members cross the line."

"He knows I plan to attend our clan meeting before coming to see him. It is possible that a cooler head within his pack has talked him into waiting until Monday as we specified."

"Unlikely. I fully expect him to do something underhanded to tip negotiations in his favor. You need to take every precaution while you're there."

"I will be careful." Edrigu could be a worrier. But more often than not, his fears had merit.

"You should take Ganix with you when you meet with him. You need someone to watch your back."

"I appreciate your concern, but I've been watching my back for more than a century now. Besides, Valter cannot start a fight while I'm here without repercussions from the families, the packs, and Tullamore itself."

"A bunch of humans cannot stop a rogue shifter bent on revenge."

"There aren't just humans on staff here. You know that."

"Bah. Just stay alert."

"How is Palben?" Amarande asked, changing the subject. He had been worried about Edrigu's son since he first heard he had been attacked by shifters.

"About the same. Ler found a way to get a small amount of bagged blood into him, but I don't think it's enough."

"I suspect this attack left more than physical wounds." Everything the girls had told him about Palben's recovery made him wonder if the boy suffered from emotional wounds.

"I do too. The only thing I am grateful for is that he is still too weak to chase down those shifters and exact any form of revenge."

"That would be unwise." Palben normally demonstrated good sense but emotion often overruled logic after trauma.

"For more than one reason. Which is why I greatly appreciate you offering to intervene in the situation."

Amarande dipped his head. "I promise I will find a satisfactory resolution, no matter what."

Edrigu grasped Amarande by the shoulder. "There is no one I trust more to handle this than you."

Pride that his sire still trusted him so much made him stand even taller. "Thank you. I won't let you down."

Edrigu nodded then went to the bar to pour himself a drink. "I just hope that whatever is blocking Palben's ability to heal is resolved before you meet with them."

"Could he be grieving the loss of the girl?" He had been gone long enough that he didn't know the girl who had been with Palben when he was attacked. After making a few discreet inquires, he had learned she was shifter and allegedly had sought Palben's help.

"Ridiculous." Edrigu splashed some of the amber liquid into a crystal glass. "She isn't worth his life."

"He may disagree with that sentiment."

"She wasn't even vampire." Edrigu's roar echoed through the room.

Amarande felt the familiar tingle in his gums as his fangs threatened to lengthen. His nostrils flared as he drew in a steadying breath to quell his instinct to attack something. Edrigu's outbursts did not always mean an attack. But lately, his own anger lurked too close to the surface for comfort and had burst out at inappropriate times. "Evangeline and Bodgir's coupling proves that isn't a requirement." Amarande took another cleansing breath and added, "Give him time. Perhaps he will come around now that he's had some blood."

"We'll see." Weariness and maybe even a touch of fear echoed in Edrigu's voice.

Once again Amarande changed topics. "I assume you plan to attend the welcome reception?"

"Yes. It would be considered rude to do otherwise."

"Shall I return to escort you and Shaia?"

"You're here for the bachelor race, are you not? There is no need for you to escort me anywhere." Edrigu patted him on the shoulder. "The ladies and their patriarchs need to see you operating independently of my influence. Anything else will weaken your chances."

"I've been operating independently of you for some time now."

"I know that but some of the older, more remote clan leaders may not."

He dipped his head. "Very well. I will see you there then."

"Yes." Edrigu followed him to the suite door. "Oh and Amarande? Watch your back this weekend. You never know how far the bachelorettes or your competitors would be willing to go to eliminate anyone they see as a threat. As soon as all of the bachelor names are announced tonight, it will be open season. Don't let yourself be caught exposed."

He relished the thought of such a challenge, but Edrigu didn't need to know that. Amarande had surprised himself by how dark his thought had been turning of late. "I'll be careful."

"Good." He patted Amarande on the back. "But be sure to save Shaia one dance tonight. She will be disappointed if you do not."

Amarande smiled. Shaia was a special lady. Edrigu had captured one of the only gems in the realm when he mated with her. "Give her my best when she wakes and tell her she can have any dance she wishes."

"I will do that."

Only after Edrigu closed the door did Amarande allow himself to breathe a sigh of relief. He hated withholding information from his sire. But in this instance it was for the best. He hadn't lied to Edrigu, but he didn't tell him the whole truth. While he hadn't spoken with Valter, Valter's second had sent a message saying they would meet him later tonight to discuss details of his meeting with the pack leader.

Thankfully Edrigu was still too preoccupied with Palben's condition to pick up on his omission of truth.

After cleaning up and changing into a fresh suit Amarande made his way downstairs. According to the itinerary, a welcome reception was being held in one of the ballrooms. After being cooped up in the car for so long on the drive to Tullamore, it would be good to stretch his legs. And the idea of a drink or two held considerable appeal.

When he reached the hotel lobby, he asked one of the porters for directions to the appropriate room. He followed the young man through three different stone passageways until they reached a series of doors. Just inside the door a young woman stood at the ready with some kind of electronic device in hand. Based on the dark blue suit she wore, Amarande guessed her to be some kind of hotel management but the flash of fang when she spoke made him second guess that. "Good evening, sir. May I have your name, please?"

"Amarande Maniaci."

"Good evening, Mr. Maniaci." She tapped something into her device. When she looked up again her eyes held a distinct flicker of interest. "Is anyone joining you this evening?"

"Only if the evening goes well."

Her gaze strolled across his chest and lower before returning to her device. She clicked one last button then motioned toward the ballroom doors. "You'll find the bar along the wall on your left. Hor d'oeuvres will be circulating through the room."

He dipped his head in acknowledgement.

"And if there is anything I can do to make your evening more..." She licked her lips. "...enjoyable don't hesitate to ask."

"Thank you." He checked her name tag then added, "Tammy."

With one last cursory glance to see if anything about the woman sparked his interest, he glided through the doors being held open by two attendants. There was a point in his life where he would have taken full advantage of the woman's interest in him and filled his nights by exploring the many ways they could pleasure each other. While those interludes had been exciting, they ultimately left him empty. When your soul craved a deep and honest connection, pleasures of the flesh paled in comparison.

Yet here he was, nearly three hundred years old, without a heartmate.

Throughout his vampire existence Edrigu had told him stories of what he could expect when he found his heartmate. How to recognize her. And how his life would change once he did.

But not everyone found their heartmate. Many vampires settled for companionship. But after living with Edrigu since his youngling stages and seeing what a heartmate relationship could be like anything else was unpalatable.

Edrigu had been one of the fortunate ones. His heartmate, Shaia, had come to him when they were both younglings. They spent the better part of their lives together. Edrigu was fiercely protective of Shaia, and she of him. Their love, even now, was a tangible thing.

That was what Amarande wanted.

That was what he craved.

After decades of looking for her, he doubted whether he would ever find his heartmate. He had searched multiple countries and come in contact with very nearly every known Vampire clan yet he still had not found the one who had the power to make his blood surge. Because of that failure, he finally agreed to participate in the Bachelor Trials. It would be the largest gathering of unmated females for the next century. Therefore, his best chance at finding his heartmate.

If he didn't find her here, he would be forced to settle for companionable love. Anything to keep the darkness from smothering the last of his humanity.

He snagged a glass from the tray of a passing server and downed the contents of his drink in one swallow in an effort to shake off the depressing thought. Normally he didn't dwell on what he had already determined to be his fate. For some reason this trip had driven home how empty his life had become.

He scanned the room.

As expected, very few of the attendees were human. The ones who were there very obviously belonged with one of the vampire sires. Likely either as a blood pet or bonded assistant.

One of his former colleagues chatted amicably with a group of men. The poor bastards probably didn't know she was capable of ripping their spine out without breaking a sweat. He chuckled. He would actually love to see her in a training ring against any one of them. Sober or drunk.

He lifted his empty glass in a salute as he passed her ring of admirers. She winked at him in response making more than one of her admirers look his way.

When he drew near the bar he sensed a shifter's presence. He discretely scanned the area looking for the source. He spotted a man towering over one of the vampiresses he had briefly met at one of the regional clan meetings. Given the man's stature he suspected he hailed from one of the extremely rare bear packs in the area.

After getting a real drink from the bar Amarande drifted closer so he could better catch the man's scent. The pungent scent of pine and animal fur confirmed his suspicions that the man was indeed a bear shifter.

Unless Valter had far more influence than they knew, the bear shifter should pose no threat. Based on the way the vampiress gazed up at him adoringly, she was likely the reason he attended the function. Even the bear's stoic expression softened when he looked down at her.

"Good evening, everyone."

Amarande halted his exploration of the attendees and turned toward the microphone.

Gaspard, one of Lord Edrom's sons, addressed the crowd from the raised platform at the front of the room. "I hope everyone is having a pleasant evening."

There were murmurs of agreement from the crowd.

He turned as he spoke. "I see many familiar faces and a few I have yet to meet. Father and I are both pleased that you were all available to join us this year."

The crowd clapped politely.

"I just wanted to thank you for coming and to introduce a few key people, for those of you who haven't had an opportunity to meet them yet." Gaspard gestured to a gray headed and bearded man not far from him.

"I'm sure almost all of you know Robert Villauhague. He is, in my opinion, the best mage on the continent. And perhaps even the globe. His reputation for fairness is untarnished and we're lucky he was able to join us this weekend. Be sure to introduce yourself before the evening is over." He held up one finger. "And for those of you wishing to get on his good side, he only drinks Irish whiskey. None of that foreign stuff."

Chuckles and applause came from the crowd.

As Amarande listened to Gaspard give what amounted to a political speech, he sensed someone approaching from behind. He turned slightly to get a look and ready his attack if needed.

Always prepared.

The heavy scent of jasmine and bergamot wafted through the air. Amarande had no doubt about who approached. Kesila, Lord Edrom's daughter, was a much cherished, yet somewhat spoiled, young woman who rode the coattails of her well-positioned and powerful father whenever she could. She might be a perfect example of vampire beauty but she was, without a doubt, a pain in the ass.

"I see Ed decided to send a friendly face this year." Kesila ran her finger across his shoulders as she passed behind him.

Her high-handed attitude had not changed in the last decade. "Actually Lord Moreschi didn't send anyone. If he isn't here already, he will be shortly."

"Oh really? The old man decided to grace us with his presence. Father will be pleased, I suppose."

Amarande tamped down his annoyance at her disrespect for his sire and refrained from commenting. Edrigu had never hidden his disdain of Kesila and the two always seemed to butt heads. When Amarande had been Edrigu's second, he ran interference whenever he could. But since he had moved into the ranks of Enforcement, it was no longer his place to do so. So if she wanted to risk irritating the second most powerful vampire in their world, it would be on her to get out of trouble.

"It's good to see you, Amarande," she purred. "I hear you have done well with the Enforcers. And I can see for myself that all that hard work looks good on you. I do hope to see more of you this weekend."

He turned to take a better look at her. She had always made it clear that she would welcome an attachment with him. But as before, his heart did not pound, nor did the blood in his veins sing. He knew from the moment they had met that she was not the one for him.

If he decided to give up the pipe dream of finding his heartmate and simply look for a strategic alignment, she would certainly be a viable option. After all, he had not dismissed the idea of becoming a clan leader at some point. "Perhaps you shall."

She smiled seductively as she ran one red-tipped finger down the front of his crisp white shirt. "I look forward to it." Then she slipped back into the crowd, most likely to find her next potential victim.

3

REAGHAN took the hand of the porter who greeted her at the castle entrance. He helped her out of the back of the limousine Caoilfhinn had conjured for her to use after portaling through to the human realm. "Welcome to Tullamore."

"Thank you." She gazed up at the stone structure with a degree of trepidation. When she realized she was just short of gawking, she stepped out of the porter's way so he could retrieve her things from inside the car.

"Do you have luggage, miss?" the porter asked.

"Just the one." She gestured to the bag he already held. "I'll take my case though if you don't mind." She took the curved case protecting her violin from harm.

"Right this way, Miss." He led her to the massive wood doors that guarded the entrance to the hotel. By human standards they probably seemed timeless. However, to her they were just one more human relic left to mark the passage of time. The carvings were however beautiful and expertly crafted.

The doors opened allowing the dry, interior air the freedom to ripple across her skin. She followed the porter to the registration desk. He set her bag on one of the bellhop carts. "Someone will be right with you."

Reaghan smiled at the young man and handed him a few folded bills. "Thank you so much."

He touched the brim of his cap. "My pleasure, Miss." Then he hurried back to his station at the front door.

A woman with red hair, wearing a prim suit, looked up from her work at the desk. "Good evening. Miss McCarthy, by chance?"

Reaghan blinked back her surprise. "Yes."

The woman smiled. "Excellent. I'm Alanna Byrne. Welcome to Tullamore."

Reaghan took Alanna's offered hand. She experienced a brief moment of nervousness at meeting the infamous guardian of Tullamore. "It's lovely to finally meet you in person."

Alanna raised a brow. "Finally?"

"My cousin, Carol Mulrooney, told me so many stories of the property and the people here that I feel like I know everyone." Where Caoilfhinn came up with her human name, she'd never know. But Reaghan wasn't above dropping it when needed.

Alanna's smile widened. "Oh, yes, Carol. We have loved having her pop in over the years." She leaned closer. "Tell me, did she and that handsome young man she last visited with ever tie the knot?"

"They did. It was a lovely wedding."

"Good. Be sure to tell her that we'd love to host her and her husband for an anniversary getaway."

"I will tell her." Reaghan smiled pleasantly even though she couldn't imagine the king and queen taking a short holiday. Then again, they might need one after their current emergency was resolved.

"As a relative of Carol's, we're even more happy to have you stay with us. I hope your journey to Tullamore was pleasant?"

"Indeed. Thank you." A quick step through a portal was far easier than travelling in a human automobile or airplane but she couldn't say that.

"Good. I know that Noémie, Lord Edrom's assistant, was quite relieved when you agreed to come at the last minute for their event. I, for one, am quite anxious to hear you play."

"Thank you. While I was sad to hear that Signore Mengoni had become ill, I was flattered to be invited. Have you any word on his condition?" Even though she knew whatever illness Caoilfhinn had inflicted on the poor man wouldn't be life threatening, asking about him was the polite thing to do. By human standards, anyway.

"Only that his doctor and voice coach have forbidden him from speaking above a whisper for the next week."

"I do hope it is nothing serious and that he recovers quickly."

"As do we all. Now…" Alanna placed a few printed pages on the counter. "Everything has been prepared for your stay. There is a map of the hotel and the agenda provided by Noémie. She asked me to tell you that she will drop by your room as soon as she is free after tonight's event." Alanna typed a few things in the computer then looked over her wire rimmed glasses. "I'm afraid the welcome reception started more than an hour ago."

Reaghan waved her hand. "That's all right. I'm a little tired after my trip anyway." Although she hated missing the opportunity to look for Eirin right away.

Alanna's raised brow reminded her of one of her childhood teachers. A severe woman who tolerated no nonsense from anyone. Alanna placed two more sheets of paper in front of Reaghan. "I just need your signature here and here." She glanced at the luggage cart the porter had rolled to the end of the counter. "Just the two items to go up to your room?"

"Yes."

"I'll ring for one of the…" Alanna's sentence trailed off as something across the lobby caught her attention.

Reaghan turned to see what had distracted her so.

A rather intriguing man had taken a seat in one of the seating areas just inside lobby. He was lovely specimen. The air around him flickered with tiny bursts of energy cautioning her he wasn't human. Based on his poise and grace, unless she was very much mistaken, he was an ancient creature. His clothing spoke of money well spent. Power poured off of him but so too did weariness.

Her senses whispered vampire, making her entire body tense. Given that the hotel was likely full of vampires, it was a reasonable assumption.

Despite her wariness, she found herself drawn in his direction before she realized it. Odd that her heart pounded for reasons other than fear when she looked at him.

Alanna cleared her throat. "Excuse me." Her smile seemed forced and she rushed through the rest of her greeting. "I'll get one of our bellhops to take your things and show you to your room. Please don't hesitate to let us know if there is anything you need during your stay."

Reaghan blinked to clear her thoughts. "Yes. Thank you I will."

Alanna's sights were set on the vampire as she hurried around the corner of the desk in his direction.

Reaghan tracked Alanna's movement toward the front door. She said something to the two porters standing at attention by the door but kept shooting glances at the man in the chair. More specifically, at the three men who had entered the hotel and approached the man in the chair.

The three men also sparkled with magical energy, but theirs differed from the vampire. Shifters? Her senses said wolf shifters, to be exact.

The men fanned out, forming a semicircle around the one she suspected to be a vampire. Instead of being alarmed by the shifters' obvious attempt at intimidation he stared at the point man with an expression of utter boredom. Words were exchanged but before she could tune into what they were saying the porter arrived.

"I have your bags, Miss McCarthy. If you'll follow me."

"Oh, yes, of course." Reaghan's gaze dropped to the porter's hand. She gestured to her violin. "I'll take that one."

"It's no trouble, Miss."

"I'm sure it's not, but I'd feel more comfortable carrying it, myself." She returned the porter's pleasantries, but her attention kept returning to the vampire and the shifters.

Alanna had made her way to where they were grouped together. With only a few words she sent the three men on their way, out of the hotel.

"The lift is here, Miss," the porter reminded her.

She glanced behind her one more time. "Thank you." She stepped into the metal box as he held the doors open for her. When she turned and faced the lobby again she found the vampire had gotten to his feet and was staring intently at her.

Their eyes met.

A wave of cold washed over her, but a flood of warmth immediately followed it. Her heart skipped a beat and her breath caught in her throat.

Surprise crossed his otherwise emotionless face.

If she wasn't mistaken, in the split second that it had taken for them to notice each other, the vampire stepped in her direction. Their connection was abruptly cut off when the doors slid shut. She shivered at the loss.

What was that about? She slumped against the wall of the elevator box.

"Are you all right, Miss?" the porter asked

"Yes." She touched the side of her head and gave him a shaky smile. "I believe my travels have finally caught up to me though."

He nodded in understanding. "That happens sometimes."

The doors to the elevator opened. "This is your floor, Miss. Do you need assistance?"

"No. I'm fine. Truly."

He looked as if he didn't completely believe her but he gestured to the left. "Your room is just this way."

"Thank you." She crossed her arms over her belly and rubbed her hands up and down her arms where the tingle from that temporary connection lingered.

She didn't have time to be distracted from her mission by a handsome face. Especially when that handsome face belonged to a vampire.

Eirin was her priority.

She'd only let a handsome face distract her once before. And she'd never forgotten what happened when that vampire had gotten too close. She touched the place on her shoulder and shivered.

Never again.

4

AMARANDE tried to focus on what Alanna was saying but he was too stunned.

The faint echo of a heartbeat still thrummed in his ears. How was that possible? Only a heartmate could bring a vampire's blood to life.

Who was that woman? Was she a guest? If so, he might have a chance of finding her again. Maybe then he could figure out why he reacted so strongly to her.

"I'm afraid, Mr. Maniaci, that I must remind you Tullamore is neutral ground." Alanna's voice finally broke through his thoughts. "Any violation of that rule will result in all parties being banned from the property. Meeting or no."

He faced Alanna. "I understand completely and have no intention of violating your rules. My stay here is not meant to begin or continue any disputes. Tonight's meeting was simply to reassure those…gentlemen that I had arrived and to negotiate suitable transportation for after the meetings here at the hotel."

"Will there be future visits from them or any other members of their…" Alanna glanced around her. "Of their family?"

"Not that I have been made aware of. I will meet with them after this weekend's events."

Alanna opened her mouth but Amarande quickly added, "Off Tullamore land, of course."

She gave him a sharp nod. "Then I'll bid you goodnight."

"Good night to you."

He smoothed the line of his suit jacket as he watched Alanna walk away. As soon as she rounded the corner of the hotel desk his gaze returned to the elevator doors. Part of him longed to scale the side of the lift and ascertain which floor the mysterious woman had disembarked on but what good would that information do him?

Alanna would know her name and which room she was staying in. If he could persuade her to share it. He dismissed that idea as soon as it entered his head. Alanna had an eerie way of knowing too much about her guests. He wasn't about to confirm his interest in one of them.

Besides, he was perfectly capable of finding a single human on his own.

Then again, why would a human be here if not for the meeting? He frowned. Normally the clan meeting filled all of the guest rooms. Could she be associated with one of the attendees?

Dark thoughts clouded his mind. To the point that his fangs elongated.

He headed toward a less crowded wing of the castle but he couldn't stop the flood of images in his mind's eye of the woman being embraced by some unknown dark figure. Her pale blond hair splayed across someone's pillow. Her creamy flesh being pierced by a set of fangs.

His attitude deteriorated rapidly because of some unknown woman who may or may not be involved with someone else. He needed to get away before he lashed out at someone who didn't deserve it. Not only would it be illogical, but also impair his chances at the bachelor challenges.

When he passed the emergency staircase, he rushed through the door and hurried up to the roof. Without a thought he managed the locks and made his way to the railing at the edge. The cold night air cooled his temper to the point that he could breathe easy. His reaction to a complete stranger was nothing short of irrational.

Perhaps he should talk with Edrigu.

He grimaced. Edrigu had enough to worry about with Palben's health. He wasn't about to add to his stress. He could figure this out on his own.

It was possible that he had imagined the heartbeat. There had been so much talk about heartmates recently that he could be jumping at shadows.

He took a few more cleansing breaths then returned to the main floor. It was nearly time for him to join the council and see who the other bachelors were. After seeing them at the welcome reception, he expected Inigo and Dunixi to be in the group. But he wasn't sure about any others.

Edrigu had already told him that the original pool of interested parties had been far larger than they expected. Which was why the council had agreed to implement an updated version of games they used centuries ago to determine who would make a good mate. Males and females alike would compete to show off their skills and abilities.

For the first time in a long while, he had a suitable challenge to look forward to.

He headed to The Dungeon, the bar in the lowest level of the castle, to kill some time. Perhaps he would be able to pick out a few more of the competitors. After decades of working with the Enforcers, he believed in reconnaissance and preparation.

He chose a dark corner where he could keep an eye on the primary bar as well as a good portion of the room. From there he nursed a whiskey and kept a close watch on those who came and went. Particularly the small group of cocky males who were tossing back drinks like they were free.

Vampires might have an accelerated metabolism, but in his opinion, heavy drinking before an important meeting like this one spoke either of overconfidence or insecurity. Based on the behaviors he observed from that group it seemed to be a dangerous combination of both.

His phone buzzed, drawing his attention. He checked the message and learned the council was requesting all bachelors report to one of the meeting rooms.

A cheer went up from the group at the bar. Amarande waved the server over.

"What else can I get you?"

"For my drink and a little assistance." Amarande handed him a twenty pound note. "What's the fastest route to this meeting room?" He showed the young man his phone message.

"That's two levels up." The server considered the question then added, "When you leave, take a left and use the lift at the end of that corridor instead of going back toward the lobby. Hit two. When you get off the lift, you should be just around the corner from that meeting room."

"Much obliged."

He waited until the crowd thinned then headed to the elevator his server had suggested.

When he arrived at the proper meeting room, he slipped to the back of the room and watched the others shake hands and kiss the asses of the council lords.

Finally, Lord Edrom greeted the group as a whole. "Good evening, everyone. Thank you for responding to our message so quickly. We asked you here so that we could review the rules for this weekend's event. But we also thought you should have a chance to find out who your competitors were."

There were noises of agreement from some of the attendees.

Lord Edrom went on, "In addition, we the council lords, thought it would be good to speak with each of you, in an effort to get to know you better. Or in some cases, to put a face with a name." He gestured to his left. "But first, let me introduce Noémie. She is my personal assistant. If you have questions or issues related to schedules or challenges, please funnel them through her. She's going to cover the rules related to the challenges as well as the expectations for this weekend."

Noémie stepped up next to Lord Edrom and went through whatever she had written on her clipboard. As expected, the use of magic during any of the challenges was forbidden. He listened with half an ear as he studied the other contestants. Under the best circumstances, the ratio of bachelors to bachelorettes was near to even. This time, the bachelors far exceeded the bachelorettes. If he wanted to be in a position to have the mate of his choosing, he would need to maintain absolute focus and clarity.

None of those hovering near the front gave him any sense of alarm or that they would present any sort of challenge. Unless they opted for cheating and deception. The thought of dealing with a cheating entrant gave him a small measure of pleasure.

He continued to assess the crowd until he spotted a few people he recognized. Two were drop outs from the early phase of Enforcer training. Doubtful they would pose any challenge.

The man standing just to their left, however, would be a formidable opponent. Willem had been second to Lord Adenauer until a northern clan overtook his. He had been instrumental in negotiating the peace treaty but when the dust settled, he agreed to leave so the other clan's second could step up. Since then he had been building a personal security business catering to wealthy humans and non-humans alike. He would certainly be a worthy challenger.

Amarande smiled in anticipation.

There were a few others in the group he would like to have more information about. As much as it went against his norm, it might be worthwhile to talk with the competitors he knew.

"Now that the business side has been covered, we will begin the interviews." Lord Edrom nodded to the other council lords who were gathered off to his right. "When Noémie calls your name, step into the adjoining room. Each interview should only take five minutes, depending on how many questions the council has for you. Once your interview is concluded you are free for the evening." He gestured to his assistant. "Noémie, if you will." She took her place at the door while Lord Edrom followed the last council lord through the doors behind them.

"We will be calling candidates in alphabetical order, based on first names." She glanced at her list. "Amarande Maniaci."

A hush descended over the room as he stepped out of the shadows. The crowd ahead of him parted to allow him through.

He spotted more than one stunned expression as he passed. A few others were clearly disappointed to see him in their ranks. He smiled knowing there were some surprised to see how far a turned vampire had climbed in their ranks. It really was too bad he couldn't hear the comments after he left. Perhaps Willem would enlighten him later.

The doors to the meeting room closed behind him. He took the next step toward achieving his primary goal and calmly faced the council.

 5

THE next day, Reaghan had a light luncheon then dressed to go down to the castle auditorium to rehearse before any of the vampires were up. She didn't require much sleep in the human realm. And, in truth, she was anxious to complete her mission. So she might as well put her time to good use.

She was scheduled to play later that evening after dinner. Despite not having played for anyone other than her family in some time, she wasn't worried. Her skill on the violin, by human standards was exceptional. And if boosted with a touch of power, could mesmerize anyone she desired. But the practice gave her an excuse to move about the meeting spaces unaccompanied and fell in line with her cover story of a human musician.

As expected, the ballroom was empty, save for a few hotel employees who were busy cleaning and setting the room for the next event.

She took her instrument out and ran her hands over the polished wood lovingly as memories of her first lessons surfaced. Her brother had surprised her by arranging for her to take lessons from a friend of a friend, one of the early masters, as part of her first trip into the mortal plane. Once she mastered it, her father obtained a violin made by Nicola Amati. It was his way of supporting her talent even though her mother disapproved of anything human. But even her mother had been caught enjoying the sound of her music.

To warm up her fingers and ensure everything was properly tuned, she played one of her favorite songs. Then, leaving her shoes next to the chair, she twirled about the room while practicing the ones she wanted to play for Lord Edrom. Dancing gave her a chance to not only check the room's acoustics, but to search for traces of fae magic.

She detected trace amounts of magic, but it was so diluted with residual energy from the other beings that she couldn't pin point its origins.

Perhaps she would be able to trace it outside of the ballroom after she had finished.

She finished her exploration of the room then returned to the chair in the center of the dance floor. After making a couple of adjustments to her violin she dove into one of her hardest pieces. She closed her eyes and let herself be swept away with the music. Her bow moved across the strings almost of their own accord. During the last half of the song a man added his voice to the song. It should have surprised her, but the sound blended in so smoothly that it just felt...right. Her music sparkled and flowed like never before and dragged her further into the spell she had inadvertently woven.

When the last note was played it lingered in the room like an endless echo. She opened her eyes and found the man from the lobby standing near the edge of the wood floor.

The expression on his face was intense. As if he could devour her whole while making her enjoy it. And yet she sensed a touch of awe, as if he couldn't quite believe what he was seeing. It stirred a warmth not only within her body, but also her soul.

Their gazes met. She couldn't have looked away even if the building caved in. The connection she felt the last time she saw him sizzled to life. It sparked a flame within her that took on a life of its own. The warm feeling bubbled quickly spread throughout her body.

"Brava!" An older man called from the door. He clapped his hands as he and Noémie, Lord Edrom's assistant, entered the room, breaking the spell their music had woven. She chanced a glance at the mystery man while the older man hobbled to the edge of the dance floor, leaning heavily on his cane. "That was simply beautiful." He held out his hand to Reaghan. "Noémie tells me you are Mademoiselle McCarthy."

Reaghan transferred her bow into her other hand before shaking his. "I am."

"I am Lord Edrom."

"Oh, yes." She dipped her head respectfully. "I am flattered that you thought of me for your event."

"You have my wife to think for that." He smiled. "She is quite the fan."

"Then I am doubly pleased." She risked another glance at the vampire hovering to her left.

"And you, Amarande." Lord Edrom turned his assessing glaze on the mystery man. "I haven't heard you sing in some time. It seems our guest has inspired you."

The man gave Lord Edrom a stiff smile. "It would appear so."

Lord Edrom's gaze danced between them. "You two have met before, yes?"

Reaghan shook off the effects of their initial contact. "Yes." She pulled her violin close to her chest. "I mean, no."

Lord Edrom raised a brow in question.

"I mean," She gestured at the man. "I saw you in the lobby last night as I was checking in but we were not introduced."

"Ah." Lord Edrom nodded. "Then allow me." He gestured to the taller vampire. "This is Amarande Maniaci. He is one of our clan's up and coming." To Amarande he added, "And this, as you already learned, is Mademoiselle McCarthy, our guest musician."

Reaghan offered her hand to Amarande. "It's nice to meet you." When their hands touched a wave of electricity passed through her. Her lips parted on a gasp but he tightened his grip and wouldn't allow her to pull away.

Instead of shaking her hand, he bowed slightly over it. "I assure you, the pleasure is all mine." Unless she was very much mistaken the color of his eyes changed from the palest blue to sparkling turquoise. "Your playing is magnificent. I hope you didn't mind my joining in so unexpectedly. I found that I could not resist."

His voice rippled across her skin like a lover's caress. The urge to rub her body against his burned within her. "No, I...I don't mind at all," she reassured him. "It appears your voice is the perfect complement to my violin."

"I just had an excellent notion. The two of you should do a duet at tonight's dinner." Lord Edrom glanced at his assistant as if looking for confirmation of his idea. She quickly nodded her agreement. "I'll leave it to you two to work out the details but I expect to hear you lend your voice for at least one song." He gestured to Amarande with the hand holding the cane. "I believe the council and the rest of our guests would be pleasantly surprised to learn of your hidden talent, Amarande. If you know what I mean?"

"I'd be happy to join Mademoiselle McCarthy, so long as she

does not object."

Her heart skipped in her chest at the thought of spending time with a vampire who was far too handsome for her comfort. Still, she was a diplomat, so she pasted a smile on her face. "I believe we can work something out."

Lord Edrom rapped his cane on the wood floor with a thump. "Then we will leave you to it. Come, Noémie, I would like to speak with Mistress Alanna about something."

"Yes, your lordship." Noémie dipped her head to Reaghan and Amarande in parting then hurried after Lord Edrom.

Reaghan faced Amarande and was once again unsettled by the intensity of his gaze. "I, uh…I hope Lord Edrom didn't mind my using the ballroom to practice. I thought, given the lateness of your event last evening, that no one would be about for a few more hours."

"Lord Edrom is known for being an early riser," Amarande told her.

She tipped her head to one side. "You as well?"

"When I have things on my mind. Or tasks to accomplish."

Without turning her back to the unsettling vampire, she retrieved her case and added the precious instrument. Much to her chagrin, her jittery nerves made her hands tremble. "And which of those had you leaving the comfort of your bed early?"

"Both."

She flipped the latch on her case then picked it up by the handle.

Amarande immediately moved closer with his hand outstretched. "Allow me."

Even though his old-world manners pleased her, she shook her head. "Normally, I wouldn't argue when a gentleman offers to carry my things, but this…" She lifted the case just enough to draw attention to it. "This is one of the few exceptions."

He folded his hands behind his back. "I understand your reluctance. I feel the same about a few of my weapons."

"Just to be clear, I didn't decline your offer for fear that you might kill me with my violin."

One side of his lips twitched into a partial smile. It was, however, the twinkle in his eye that melted part of the defensive barrier she had raised upon meeting him. How did this man affect her so? She started for the exit in an attempt to regain control of her wayward emotions.

"There are few people in this world able to kill me. Much less with one of my own weapons. I simply do not trust anyone with the handling and care of them."

"Are your weapons delicate then?" She was probably pushing her luck with this vampire but she simply couldn't resist teasing him.

"Hardly. I am a collector of ancient weapons of war. I own many items that I've been told belong in a museum."

"Ah."

"Have you taken lunch yet?" he asked.

She glanced his way. "I ate not long before I left my room."

"Would you care to join me for coffee then? We should probably discuss the music you'll be playing. It would be wise, I think, to see if there is anything we could agree on before Lord Edrom decides for us."

"He did strike me as the type to take control of things."

"That's putting it nicely."

She shouldn't accept his offer, but didn't have an excuse for not. And if she were completely honest, a small part of her wanted to. Yet, she didn't know why. Besides, it might give her an opportunity to look for Eirin. "Very well. I assume there is somewhere in the hotel that serves coffee?"

"There is a café on the main floor."

She nodded. "I'd like to leave my violin in my room first. Shall I meet you at the café in about ten minutes?"

"I'll walk with you."

Butterflies fluttered about her belly and she became momentarily lost for words. When they reached the lift at the end of the corridor they both reached for the button. A surge of warmth spread through her body when their hands touched. They both froze and stared at each other.

The turquoise flecks in his eyes darkened, drawing her into the seemingly bottomless pools.

"Odd, that," she murmured.

"Indeed."

The bell dinged signaling the lift's arrival.

"I, uh… we should probably go." Her feet felt rooted to the spot and she hesitated breaking their connection.

"Yes." He cleared his throat. "After you."

Her pulse pulsed through her veins as she stepped into the tiny box.

"What floor?" he asked.

"Fifth."

He pressed the appropriate button. "We're on the same floor."

"Are we?" Why could she not control the fluttering in her belly? She'd trained for centuries to control her emotions. It would seem that had been for naught.

When the lift stopped they both exited.

"This way." She gestured to her left. "Where is your room?" She asked over her shoulder as she led the way.

"On the other side of the castle." He pointed behind them. "The other elevator is more convenient to access my suite."

Relief swamped her. Given how much he affected her with so little contact, it likely would have been distracting to know he was only a few doors away.

When they reached her room, she used her card to release the lock. "I just need a moment to set my things down and get my purse but you're welcome to wait inside."

He followed behind her then stopped near the couch and looked around. She hurried to the bedroom.

From the sitting room he called out, "Aren't you afraid of inviting a man you barely know into your room?"

"No." Not entirely true. She ran her fingers through her hair then grabbed a dainty purse that had been included in her human possessions. When she returned to the sitting room she added, "I usually have pretty good instincts about people." He turned away from the window to face her. "While I do not understand some of the things I have been feeling since I first saw you, I do not believe that you mean to harm me." As she spoke the words she realized it was true.

He quickly closed the distance between them. "You would be correct."

With a look of sheer fascination on his face, he reached for a strand of her hair. He twisted it around his finger and slid it all the way to the end. He shook off whatever emotion he had been feeling and donned what she now suspected was a mask of civility.

There was obviously more to this vampire than he let on. What truly surprised her was her desire to learn more.

He straightened his spine even more than it already was. "So, coffee."

"Yes." Following his lead, she headed to the door. Strangely enough it didn't take much effort to produce a real smile.

6

AMARANDE'S gaze returned to Reaghan time and again. How was it possible that this tiny woman could hold the power to restore warmth to his blood? A human.

It couldn't be possible.

But he couldn't deny the intense attraction every time he looked at her. Touch only magnified it. Even stroking that lock of her hair had chased some of the chill from his veins.

He knew vampires who took human companions, but they later lamented how short lived their relationships had been. Turning humans was extremely risky and rarely attempted. Which left those vampires heart sick after the human passed away. But as far as he knew, none of those humans had been heartmates.

How old was Reaghan? Her hair was an unusual color—neither blonde nor white—so that didn't give him any clues to her age. While her face and skin were youthful her eyes hinted she had seen things in her life. Things that haunted her.

What could she have experienced in her lifetime to leave such a shadow? The urge to eradicate it bubbled inside of him. Despite the fact he didn't know her.

It was too late for him to back out of the Bachelor Trials. Even if his heartmate walked up to him right then and there, he would still have to complete the games. But if there was a chance that Reaghan was his heartmate, he didn't want to lose her.

He flexed his shoulders to release some of the tension that had been building. One thing at a time.

They strolled to the café at an easy pace. Neither of them seemed to be in a hurry to be anywhere.

"Your accent. I can't quite place it. Where are you from?" she asked.

"A small village in Northern Italy that no one has ever heard of."

"One of those places where everyone knows everyone's business because they are all related somehow?"

"Indeed. Do you speak from experience?"

Her smile widened. "I do, actually. And like you, I come from a place, I dare say, you have never been."

"Based on the way you have pronounced certain words, I would guess you come from somewhere on the green isle."

"That's a good guess." Her eyes glittered mischievously.

Normally all of his senses would be on his surroundings, constantly alert to any possibility of danger, but at the moment an unusually large part of his attention was focused solely on her. "May I ask you something?"

"Just one something?"

"Well, one somewhat important thing."

She stopped walking and looked up at him. "What is this one important thing you need to know?"

"The meetings being held here this weekend are very important. And very private. Only select people are invited to attend." He stepped closer hoping to catch some indication of whether or not she lied when she answered. "How is it that you came to be invited to perform?"

She shrugged. "I assume it is as Lord Edrom said. That his wife asked for me and when they called it happened to work out for me to attend."

"I don't believe in random chance."

She tipped her head to the side. "What worries you about my being here?"

"Do you understand what the meetings being held this weekend are for and their significance?"

"Mostly. Why?"

He leaned closer. "You understand who, or more specifically what, is in attendance?"

"I do." She smiled. "Did you think I was unaware that you, Lord Edrom, and probably most of the guests in attendance are vampires?"

He straightened and blinked back his surprise. "Yes, that was my concern."

She turned and started walking to the café again. "Well you can stop worrying. I am more than familiar with your world."

He matched his steps to hers. "You sound less than pleased by that. Why do I feel there is a story there?"

"Isn't there always?"

"Would you mind sharing yours?"

She tossed a glance his way. "Why do you want to know?"

"Because I suspect it's an interesting tale." In truth, he wanted to know everything there was to know about this woman. But she wouldn't understand that.

"It really isn't."

"Shouldn't I be the judge of that?"

"Fine." She waved one hand in the air. "For a short time, I attended one of the universities in France. My roommate there was vampire. We got along great until her brother and some of his friends came to a party at our place. One of his pals didn't like it when I declined his advances." She shivered as she recalled her attacker's face. "He chased me down in the university park and tried to rip a vein out with his teeth." She pulled the neckline of her sweater aside exposing two scars that started near her collarbone and ran down the back of her shoulder blade. Scars that were likely made by a pair of razor-sharp canine teeth.

Fury simmered in Amarande's gut. His vision darkened and red coated everything he could see. "Who was he?"

"Doesn't matter." She startled at what was likely a fierce expression. "The council passed judgement on him. The others involved served their own sentences."

He grabbed her wrist. "His name."

She tugged at his grip and returned his glare. "I'll not utter that name ever again."

The steely glint in her eyes hinted she would not budge. He would simply have to learn the story some other way. He released his hold of her arm before he did something he regretted. Like sweeping her up in his arms and locking her away some place safe until the murderous intent pulsing within him subsided.

Drawing on his training and centuries of practice, he calmed his emotions and harnessed the beast that lay just below the surface. "I'm sorry for whatever you went through. I do hope you realize that not all vampires are like that."

"I know it here." She pointed to her own forehead. "But I don't always remember that here." She touched her chest. "And it bothers me more than I say to know that a shred of fear still lingers despite the years that have passed."

"There are some things you never heal from." He glanced at her shoulder. "Even after the scars fade."

"Voice of experience?"

He dipped his head but didn't elaborate. Memories of the Fae-Vamp War still haunted him when he least expected it. You would think that after more than three hundred years, they would have faded. But he could still smell the smoke and blood soaked earth where his family and friends had been slaughtered.

He forced those thoughts aside as they entered the lobby. "The café is just over there." He gestured to the area he meant.

When they reached the café they both ordered drinks then found a table along the wall, near the front. The three other patrons in the café were human. Based on their modes of dress, Amarande guessed they were likely hotel staff.

"Lord Edrom indicated he hadn't heard you sing for some time. Does that mean you have sung for a group before?" she asked.

"I have."

"Tell me about it." Her almost imperious tone didn't really fit with what he knew of the little musician, but he filed the thought away to be examined more later.

"As a child, before I was turned, I was a member of the church choir. My mother used to tell me that my singing could make the angels jealous. It was many years after her death before I ever hummed another note. When I did, my sire overheard me and insisted I entertain the family and close friends from time to time. Lord Edrom is one of the few to have been included in that group." He grinned. "But the young ones still ask me to sing them to sleep when I am home."

"That's so sweet and yet sad too."

He found he rather liked her approval. "What songs did you plan to play tonight? I only heard the one as I entered the ballroom."

"I usually play a mix ranging from classical to modern. I change it up based on how the crowd reacts."

"I shouldn't think most classical music would have accompanying lyrics."

"No. Most do not." She smiled. "Do you know any local songs?"

"Local? As in Irish?"

"Yes."

"I know a few."

She tapped on the side of her cup. "We could do a lively number and make it look as if you cannot help yourself from interrupting my playing."

He raised one brow. "Is that how you see my joining you?"

"Oh, no. I didn't mean to imply that at all." She touched his hand and his thoughts momentarily stalled. "I have seen acts do that and it's a fun way to transition into unexpected pairings."

"You think we would be unexpected?"

"Are you saying the people at this meeting would expect you to join in a singalong?"

He chuckled. "No, they would not."

"I figured as much with that if-you-look-at-me-wrong-I'll-kill-you vibe you have going on."

"I do not look like that." Did she really see him that way?

"Actually, you do."

He scowled. "Then why has no one ever told me that?"

"Probably because they're afraid you'll kill them."

He leaned forward and rested his forearm on the table. "You don't seem to be."

"On a certain level, I am, actually." She held her hand up to show him the tiny space between her thumb and first finger. "Just a little bit. But like I said earlier, my instincts keep telling me you wouldn't." She shrugged. "And at this point I'm being stubborn about not giving into my fear. It is one of the reasons I agreed to perform this weekend."

"To face your fears?" This tiny human was braver than he would have ever given her credit for. She survived a horrible experience and instead of crawling into a hole and hiding she was still trying to better herself by confronting her weakness.

She grinned as she nodded. "Plus they offered to pay me a lot of money."

He chuckled. "That probably does help." Talented, sexy, and a sense of humor. Damn. Why did she have to be mortal?

7

REAGHAN'S empty cup made a hollow thud when it rattled on the surface of the table. She was pleased they had been able to find a song they both knew well enough to perform so quickly. And, if the act went the way they discussed, it would make a good duet.

Despite how much she had begun to relax and enjoy her conversation with Amarande, she had begun to feel antsy. She needed to look for Eirin. She might be forced to play her role as the guest musician, but she had to balance that against her true purpose. And she couldn't do that sitting in a café flirting with a handsome vampire.

"Well, I—"

"Amarande!"

Her exit line was cut off by a shout from someone near the front of the café. She and Amarande both turned to see who it was.

A young man wearing jeans and a tee-shirt advertising a popular video game waved at them from his place in line. She looked at Amarande to see if he recognized him,

Amarande gave a long-suffering sigh and shook his head. "That's Paquin, one of my sire's younglings. He's a bit awkward and extremely uncoordinated but he is damn good with anything electronic."

Despite his outward appearance of annoyance, Reaghan sensed Amarande held an undercurrent of affection for the young man.

Paquin held up one finger, asking Amarande to wait for him. Amarande nodded his agreement.

"I should probably be going." She crumpled her used napkin into a ball, but Amarande lay his hand over hers, stopping her motion. The same tingling sensation she felt before when they touched skittered up her arm. Each time they touched it seemed to grow stronger.

"Please stay. I'm sure Paquin won't be here long. The boy can't sit still for five minutes at a time."

She chuckled. "Perhaps not, but I should still go."

He kept hold of her hand. It wasn't truly a restraint. He genuinely seemed loath to break their connection. "I thought you weren't expected until the dinner tonight."

"True, but I have things to do to prepare."

"Such as?"

She batted her eyelashes in an exaggerated manner. "Don't you know it takes ladies far longer to get ready for important events than men? We have hair and makeup to contend with. And don't get me started on how long it takes for nail polish to dry."

He cocked his head. "You don't strike me as the type to spend hours in the bathroom getting ready. Your natural beauty would be wasted by covering it up with a bunch of products."

She blinked. He thought she was beautiful?

She intended to create a glamour that would enable her to blend in as a human rather than stand out. The images humans considered beautiful sometimes baffled her though. Perhaps she had miscalculated this time.

"Thanks for waiting, Amarande." Paquin barely glanced in her direction, reinforcing her original assumption that her glamour was in place and suitably plain.

"Sorry for interrupting." Paquin fidgeted with his cup as he hurried through what he was saying. "I just wanted to come over and tell you good luck with the games this weekend. It's so exciting to know someone who is competing. I'm rooting for you. So are Maria and Janelle. We all hope it comes out well for you."

Amarande held up his hand. "Paquin, take a breath."

The young man complied.

"Thank you. Tell Maria and Janelle I appreciate their support when you speak with them again."

"I will. Don't worry. I—"

Amarande held up his hand again and Paquin immediately went quiet. "Paquin, this is Miss McCarthy." He gestured to her.

"Hi, Paquin." She smiled. "It's nice to meet you."

"Hi, thanks. It's nice to meet you too." As if he worried he wouldn't get it all out in a breath, Paquin rushed on. "So, Amarande,

I wanted to tell you that if you need any help with any of the games I'm here for you. Just let me know what you need. Anything at all. I can hack with the best of them. You know that. And I'm down for whatever. Okay?"

Amarande's lip twitched in amusement. "I appreciate that, Paquin. I doubt the Lords moved into the world of egames or artificial intelligence, but thank you for the offer."

"Okay, well…" Paquin's watch beeped at him, distracting him for a moment. "Ah man, I gotta run." He pushed a couple buttons on his watch as he backed away. "Just remember, I'm here if you need me." He pointed at Amarande with his coffee cup. "Anything at all you need, I'm the man."

"You're the man," Amarande repeated.

Paquin gave him a thumbs up and then hurried out of the café. He narrowly missed bumping into two people on the way out.

Amarande shook his head. "That boy," He muttered as they watched Paquin go.

"Is he always so…energetic?" Reaghan asked.

"I'm afraid so."

How did any human or in this case, vampire, constantly use so much energy? Just watching Paquin made her tired. "What are the games that Paquin mentioned you are doing?"

He leaned back in the chair and crossed his arms over his chest. He hated telling a woman he was interested in anything about what amounted to a mating ritual. "The games are what the Vampire Lords have devised to determine which of the bachelor and bachelorette vampires make a suitable mate."

Her smile faltered. "So you're hoping to find a mate then?"

He shrugged. "It was suggested to me that I was of an age where I should consider every option available to me since I had not found one yet."

"How…how many mates will you have to choose from?"

"As of last night, there were about thirty bachelors. I haven't heard an accurate count of the bachelorettes, but I understand it is considerably lower than the bachelors."

"Interesting. I never knew they held competitions to help you find a wife."

He shrugged. "Bachelor trials only occur every hundred years or so. And then only if the council deems them necessary."

She fidgeted in her seat. He was right. Despite the plausible excuse of having had a vampire roommate, she shouldn't know everything about vampires. She needed to be more careful. Something about Amarande made her want to confess her entire life story though. It was a bit unsettling. And yet, pointless. Even if she admitted to being attracted to him, it appeared that her feelings would be pointless. He was here to find a mate.

"The friend I mentioned told me a lot of things about vampires. I was around them fairly often back then." She grimaced. "Until the attack, anyway."

He looked as if he wasn't sure whether to believe her or not.

"Well, I think that it's admirable that you're willing to put yourself out there for the sake of finding the right wife. I wouldn't mind hearing more about the games but I should probably be going." She pulled her purse closer and forced a smile. "If I don't see you before your first game or event or whatever, I wish you luck." She got up to leave but he lay his hand over her wrist, effectively stopping her.

"Did I offend you in some way?"

"No." She was momentarily distracted by the zing of electricity where he touched her. "Not at all."

He gently turned her wrist, exposing her balled up fist. "Then why are you crumpling that packet of sugar and the stir stick?"

She dropped the items onto the table as if they were hot and pulled her hand away. She gave him a tight-lipped smile. "Bad habit."

From the corner of her eye she saw someone that looked like Eirin pass by the café. Her already racing heart stepped up the pace. "I...oh!" She gathered her trash and got to her feet. "I should go." She tried to get a better look at the woman without drawing attention to what she was doing.

"I thought you said you weren't offended."

"I'm not." She denied a little too brightly as she knocked her purse onto the floor.

"Then why are you in such a hurry to leave all of a sudden?"

"I, uh...I just need..." She looked over her shoulder at the café entrance. Where had Eirin gone?

Amarande stood. "Are you okay?" He handed her purse to her.

"I'm fine." She took the bag from him. "I just really need to go."

"I shall see you later this evening then."

"Hmmm? Oh, yes. Tonight." She gave him a forced smile. "I'll see you then." She hurried out the café in the direction the woman had gone. She searched the hallway as she hurried after what she quickly began to think had been a figment of her imagination.

Eirin was nowhere to be found. Nor did she detect any residue of magic. Had she just imagined seeing her?

She shook her head. Perhaps she was simply tired.

It couldn't possibly be because she was completely thrown off balance learning about the vampire dating game thing. That had nothing to do with her or her mission.

Unwilling to lose even a small chance at finding Eirin, Reaghan checked the nearby shops as well as the lobby. When she was satisfied that Eirin was nowhere to be found near the cafe, she headed to a different wing of the castle. With any luck she'd find Eirin and be able to head home earlier than planned.

Which would get her away from far too sexy vampire.

If that was what she wanted, then why did the thought of never seeing him again make her just a little bit sad?

 8

AMARANDE watched the petite human rush from the café.

He wasn't sure what he had done to upset her but as he recalled, human women were easily upset. In truth, vampire women were too. But vampire females were more likely to fight than pout. Just one of the many reasons he had avoided becoming involved with one for any length of time.

Reaghan's reaction shouldn't bother him at all. After all, they'd only just met. Yet it did.

He shook his head to clear his thoughts. He needed to focus on his primary objective of finding, if not his heartmate then at least a suitable mate. Perhaps he could find out who was left in the competition after last night's meetings. As the saying went, the best defense was a good offense.

He checked the time on his phone. He had several hours before he needed to make an appearance at any of the council meetings. Perhaps he could use the time to reacquaint himself with Lord Bromwell and Lord Vilhelm. He had met both of them years ago, but since they both live in remote regions and their clans keep largely to themselves, he had very little exposure to them. If they made the trip, surely at least one of them had a mate-able female in the games.

The only way to find out was to ask.

Edrigu's assistant would likely know where he could find them at this time of day. She was good at knowing things like that. He typed a quick message and sent it off. While he waited, he backtracked to the lobby just to give himself a destination.

"Ho, there, Amarande," someone shouted.

"Lord Grimley." He dipped his head respectfully. "How are you?"

"Good, good." The senior vampire patted Amarande on the back, turning him so they were walking in the same direction. "I was pleased to learn that you finally joined in the trials."

"You were?"

"I don't think I'm overstepping when I tell you that your interview last night went very well. The council has heard nothing but good things about your work with the Enforcers. I for one believe that if you maintain your course, you could very well advance to a Clan Leader position one day. Your extensive experience enforcing our laws would serve you and the council well."

"Thank you, my lord. I would like to think so too."

Lord Grimley shrugged one shoulder. "Not everyone believes that our Enforcers are capable of anything except following orders and killing."

"Not everyone has the privilege of working with the Enforcers. Most are too busy avoiding them."

Lord Grimley chuckled. "True."

They made their way to one of the seating areas situated off to one side of the lobby.

"I don't know if you are aware of it yet, but my clan has brought three eligible bachelorettes to the trials."

Amarande's spine straightened. "I did not realize your clan had been so blessed."

Lord Grimley shrugged. "Some say blessed. Others think the opposite."

"What do you mean?"

"Every female birth means one less male to help defend our people and our land."

"I suppose that is one way of looking at it." Amarande, however, had been raised to believe their females were as important as the males.

"As you know this weekend was made for testing the abilities of every bachelor and bachelorette in the running." Lord Grimley reached into his jacket pocket and pulled out a sheet of paper. He hesitated for a moment as if he wanted to say something more then pressed his lips together and handed the paper to Amarande. "I sincerely wish I could offer you advice on handling this challenge, but I cannot."

Amarande unfolded the sheet then turned it over to look at the back. "It's blank."

"Is it?" Lord Grimley rested his elbows on the arms of the chair and steepled his fingers in front of his face.

"Ah. Part of the challenge is to figure out how to read whatever may be printed on this."

"That is a reasonable guess."

Amarande lifted the paper so the flame of the flickering lamp on the wall behind it illuminated the page. Still nothing showed on the sheet. "Any suggestion for where to begin?"

"I'm afraid I do not."

Amarande considered the paper for a moment. "You competed for a clan leadership position, did you not, my lord?"

"I did." Lord Grimley sat back in his chair. "Several of us did." His eyes darkened. "We lost more than one leader during the war with the fae."

"Edrigu has shared many stories. Dark times."

Lord Grimley sighed. "Yes, it was. I often pray that we never know a time like that ever again." After a moment of introspection, he got to his feet. "Well, I must be off." He offered his hand to Amarande. "I wish you the best of luck this weekend."

"Thank you." Amarande grasped Lord Grimley's hand. "And thank you for this." He lifted the paper.

"You're welcome. I do hope you would consider any of our bachelorettes. I believe we could find you a comfortable place within the clan, if you so choose."

Amarande dipped his head and released Lord Grimley's hand. "I appreciate the offer and your support." He waited until Lord Grimley walked away to take a harder look at the paper.

Before he had time to study the front and back of the paper, another of the lords approached to tell him about the bachelorette from his clan. Before he could even made it out of the lobby, he'd spoken with two more lords.

Apparently, he had won the approval of at least a few of the patriarchs. Now if he and the bachelorettes in question suited then he would be in a good position.

But Reaghan...

He pushed the thought of the pale haired human aside and focused on the paper Lord Grimley had given. What he was expected to do with it? He folded it a few times and studied it from various angles but still could find no clue what he should do with it.

Who could he ask for advice? Every name he came up with made him feel as if he were trying to get someone else to solve his puzzle. He didn't want to operate that way.

Amarande took his paper and headed to the greenhouse at the rear of the castle. He did some of his best thinking while outdoors. But since it was full daylight out, he preferred to use the greenhouse in order to have a modicum of protection. At least there he could have the best of both worlds – thriving plants and areas covered by a roof.

As he navigated the main pathway through the greenhouse, he studied the parchment. He turned it every direction he could think of. He even chanted a spell he had learned some years back that would unlock charms on objects. Still nothing.

Due to the fact that he was paying more attention to what was in his hand than in front of him, when he turned a sharp corner to head to a darker area of the greenhouse, he bumped into someone.

He automatically reached to steady whoever he bumped into and was immediately assaulted by sensations. Warmth. A sweet floral scent. Reaghan. The urge to bury his face in her neck clawed at his insides.

"What...what are you doing here?" she asked in a breathless rush.

"I came out here to think." He cocked a brow. "I thought you said you have things to do before tonight's evening event."

"I do."

"Things that involve plants?"

She gave him an irritated glance. "Oddly enough, I too like to escape to the outdoors to think. My cousin's garden is one of my favorite places."

He folded the paper and tucked it into his pocket then gestured for her to precede him. Mostly as a dare. She surprised him by joining him. "And what deep thoughts are you seeking answers to?" he asked.

"Have you ever had a problem where you felt like the solution was just out of your reach?"

With his hands clasped behind his back, he strolled next to her, taking care to stay in the shadier areas. At his age, he could withstand the sun for short periods of time, but there was no sense in weakening his natural defenses when he might need them later during the physical challenge. "Yes, I have experienced that a time or two."

"I am beginning to believe I've been overthinking my problem and I need to either let it go or tackle it from a whole new angle."

Funny how he'd had the same thoughts about his own problem. "Either of those might work."

"But I'm not sure which holds the best chance of success."

"Perhaps if I knew the nature of your issue I could help."

She gave him a side-eye glance. "It's rather personal."

He shrugged. "Anything we care enough to struggle over is."

"I suppose that is true." She looked his way. "What brought a vampire out to the greenhouse during the sunniest part of the day?"

"I received a clue for one of my challenges."

"You mean one of your challenges to prove you're a worthy mate?"

"Correct."

At first her expression darkened, but then curiosity seemed to get the better of her. "So what is it?"

As much as he hated to, he admitted, "I don't know."

She frowned. "What do you mean you don't know?"

"I do not know what the challenge is. I only know it has something to do with this piece of paper." He pulled the sheet of paper from pocket and held it up in front of her.

"Does it say anything?"

He turned the paper so he could look at it again. "Not that I can see."

She peered closer. "Surely there is some kind of message on it."

"I would think so also. But if there is one, I cannot see it." Frustration pricked at his ego.

She rubbed one corner of the page between her fingers. "It feels like ordinary paper."

As soon as she touched it the paper that spot turned various shades of blue, pink, and purple. He snatched it back to see what it was doing. "What did you do?" he demanded.

Reaghan's eyes widened. "Nothing." She folded her hands to her chest. "I just felt the texture of the paper."

He shoved the paper at her. "Touch it again."

She took a step back. "I don't think—"

He wasn't above begging. "Please."

She shook her head.

He gritted his teeth and reminded himself why he shouldn't yell his frustrations at her. "Please. I need to know if there are instructions or clues or something on it. This is first time that whatever this is has done anything." He reached for her hand but she took another step away.

"Why would that be reacting to me?" She glanced at the paper as if it might explode at any second. "I have nothing to do with your challenge."

"I don't know." He growled in frustration. "Hell, I don't even know why I react to you the way I do."

She blinked in surprise. "You had a reaction to me?"

He sighed and let his hand drop.

She took a step in his direction. "How?"

The look in her eyes held such intensity, he couldn't withhold his answer. And despite his resolve to remain distant and aloof, it went against everything he stood for to lie to her. "I've felt things. When we have touched." He waited to see if she believed him but her face remained impassive. As if she had been frozen in place. "Things I haven't felt in a very long time."

"Like what?"

Their eyes met. "Warmth. The way the sun feels on your skin."

Her mouth fell open on a gasp.

"And since the first time I saw you, I can't get you out of my mind. No matter how much I try."

She looked down. Her fist opened and she spread her fingers out, palm up, as if she studied her own hand. Finally she looked up at him. "And you're here to find a mate. A vampire mate."

He winced. "Yes."

"Hmmm." She tipped her head to the side. "How old are you?"

He lifted his chin and considered whether or not she could handle the truth. If she couldn't that would be a clue that she might not be the mate he needed. "I stopped counting after I passed three hundred."

"Three hundred." She nodded. "That isn't that old."

He raised a brow doubtfully.

"For a rock."

He blinked in surprise, unsure of how to respond.

"I'm teasing you," she said with a grin. "All right. Give me the paper." She held out her hand. "I'll help you."

And with that small gesture, a ray of sunshine crept into his life.

 9

SHE took a deep breath and prayed the spell that Caoilfhinn wove to hide her magical abilities remained intact before she took the paper from Amarande. She didn't think it was possible for the paper to detect her fae magic but she wasn't certain of that. No matter what, she couldn't afford to found out this early into her trip. She still had no idea where to find Eirin.

Once again, the paper turned colors everywhere she touched it. "That's so weird."

"Are you sure you're not doing anything?" he asked.

"I'm quite sure." Her mind whirled with possibilities for why the paper changed.

"I think there is something forming in the middle."

She turned the paper so she could see. "Oh, there is. What does it say?"

"Inside."

"Is that what that word was?" she asked. "It faded before I could get a good look at it."

"I believe so."

"Your." They both spoke in unison. The word faded out like the previous.

"Heart." Once again the word faded in and then off the page.

"Lies." Reaghan swallowed the lump in her throat. Could the paper know she was lying about who she was?

"Truth." Why would it? The paper was about Amarande, not her.

They both stared at the paper waiting for the next word to appear but nothing happened.

"Is that it?" Reaghan finally asked in a hushed tone.

"I don't know." Amarande's frustration came through in his

tone.

They stared at the blank page a moment longer.

"I don't think it's going to do anything else," she suggested.

"Doesn't look like it." He sounded disappointed when he took the paper from where it rested on her open palms. Once again he inspected both sides of the sheet.

"Inside your heart lies truth. What do you think it means?" If she had to guess, the paper was trying to get him to do some introspection. But about what?

"I'm not sure." He slowly folded the paper and put it into his jacket pocket.

"So the phrase didn't mean anything to you?"

He shook his head but she could tell from his expression that his mind was racing with possibilities.

"Could it have come from a book or poem?" she suggested.

"Maybe."

"Have you ever heard that phrase before?" His distinct lack of information was starting to annoy her.

He shook off whatever he had been thinking about. "Not that I recall. But I can't discount the idea that it came from a book." He shrugged. "I've read hundreds of books in my lifetime."

Without discussing, they both headed toward the hotel entrance. After a moment he looked her way. "How old are you?"

That was definitely not something she could answer without lying. She lifted her chin defiantly. "Did anyone ever tell you it's rude to ask a lady her age?"

"Yes. But since you asked my age…" He shrugged.

"How old do you think I am?"

"I'm not a good judge of human age."

"So? Take your best guess."

"Twenty one." The way his eyes twinkled gave away the fact that he wasn't being serious.

"Not even close but we'll go with it."

He chuckled. "I'm old enough to know that it is only asking for trouble for a man to guess a woman's age."

She breathed a sigh of relief that she'd managed to dodge his question. "That's probably true." She swished her hand in the air. "You're off the hook."

"Thank you."

When they reached the lobby she automatically headed to the lift.

"Where are we going?" he asked.

"I don't know about you but I'm heading to my room."

"Ah."

She pushed the button to call the lift. "You're welcome to join me if you'd like."

His brow lifted in question. He was good at portraying a stoic hard-ass. The more she saw it the sexier it seemed to be. "I don't bite," she teased as she stepped into the lift.

"I do." He followed her into the small box.

From the intensity of the look he gave her, she couldn't tell if that was a promise or a threat. Either way, it set off flickers of warmth inside of her. She wagged a finger at him. "Yes, well you can just keep your fangs to yourself." She pressed the button for her floor. "But if you'd like a drink..." She emphasized her next words. "From the bar. And if you need to relax for a bit, you are welcome to join me. I know I could use a drink." She rubbed her belly. "Maybe some cheese too."

He slowed to match her stride as they left the lift. "I can't decide if you like dancing on the edge of trouble or just don't know when you're skirting danger."

"I thought we had already decided that you're not dangerous."

"There are a lot of vampires and quite a few others who would disagree with you."

She released the lock on her door and shot him a glance that said she was annoyed by his statement. "Not dangerous to me then."

As soon as they stepped inside her room he pushed her up against the wall making her breath catch in her chest.

His voice dropped to a husky whisper. "I don't know that I would say that at all."

Chest to chest, with his knee pressed between her legs and her wrists secured in his hand above her head, she realized she was largely at his mercy. But instead of terrifying her, as it should, it sent a dark thrill through her.

His lips grazed her cheek. As if he had all the time in the world, he buried his nose in her hair inhaled deeply. "What is it about you? I should be looking for clues to solve the puzzle for my challenge." He lifted his head and looked in her eyes. "If I fail, it will be at least one hundred years before another Bachelor Trial is held. Yet here I am. And I can think of nothing except how you would taste if I were to lay you out on the bed and lick you all over."

"I—" She swallowed the lump in her throat.

His gaze dropped to her neck. She tried to gain some kind of leverage but all she succeeded in doing was rubbing her clit against his thigh heightening the sensitivity.

"For the first time in my life, my focus is disrupted and I don't know what to do to get it back."

"Perhaps one kiss would make it all go away."

He chuckled. The gravelly sound sent a fresh set of ripples through her body. "Does that usually work for you?"

She nodded.

"I strongly suspect that won't work for me. As a matter of fact, it will probably only make things worse."

She gasped as the muscles in his thigh shifted just enough to put a little more pressure on her sensitive bud. "Worse?"

"Oh, yes. I bet you're the kind of girl that isn't easily forgotten. Whose kisses stick in your memory and haunt you in the middle of the night." He took a ragged breath then loosened his grip on her wrists.

She let her hands rest on his chest. "I, uh—"

His eyes flickered like a blue flame. "I should go."

She bit her lip, drawing his gaze.

"If I don't leave now neither of us will be leaving this room for hours. And I cannot afford to miss today's physical challenge."

"Physical?" Her voice squeaked when she asked her question.

"Mmmhmm. Very physical," he murmured.

A shiver ran through her body.

His muscles quivered, as if he struggled with his own desires. Disappointment crept in when he removed his knee from between her legs and eased her to the ground. He held on to her until she was steady on her feet. Only then did he take a step back.

She straightened her clothes, which only succeeded in keeping his attention on her.

"I'll see you this evening," he told her.

She nodded, unsure of how her voice might sound. When he reached the door, he paused and looked back at her. She held her breath waiting to see what he might do or say. It wasn't until the door clicked shut behind him that she finally allowed herself to breathe. She slumped against the wall and rubbed her hand across her face. "What the hell am I doing getting mixed up with a vampire?"

She strode into the sitting room on unsteady feet to get a drink.

She filled one of the glasses almost to the top with the wine she had opened the previous night. It took three long drinks before her hand stopped trembling. Not from fear but from unadulterated need. That realization shook her to her core.

Since her first steps into adulthood she had never felt so needy.

Her mind whispered he was a creature to be feared but her heart insisted he would never hurt her. Her traitorous body screamed she didn't care as long as he touched and licked her like he said he wanted to. Oh and as long as she had a half dozen orgasms.

Was that too much to ask?

 10

AMARANDE headed to the area of the castle where the council meetings were being held.

He needed to gather everything he could about the mysterious paper he'd been given. And he had to do something —anything— to get Reaghan out of his head.

He passed dozens of vampires coming and going from the various meeting rooms. Every room had some sort of event going on. Everything from business meetings to family or clan reunions.

Council meetings were held every ten years but the trials made this year's even more popular. Hundreds of vampires were in attendance. In many cases, council meetings were the only time clans were able to visit with distant relatives.

Technology helped narrow distances, but ten years between meetings was a long time to go without family. Even for those with extended lifetimes.

He spoke to a couple of people who stopped him as he passed. Most didn't. His reputation as one of the best Enforcers kept most at a distance.

As he talked with one of Edrigu's cousins, he noticed someone hauling a ladder through the crowded hallway. The somewhat familiar man worked quickly to change light bulbs in one section. Then he moved further down to repair a fixture. When Edrigu's cousin moved on, Amarande moved closer to see who the man was. Something about the man's movements and awareness of his surroundings that tripped memories of the many wars he had fought in.

When Amarande drew close, the man paused and turned his head ever so slightly, as if he knew he was being watched. He climbed down the ladder and returned his things to the bucket. Then he turned so Amarande could see his face. Amarande instantly shifted into defense mode.

The other man finally looked up and met his gaze. Neither man betrayed any emotion but the tension in the room spiraled up.

Amarande inched closer. "Callum. I thought you would surely be dead by now."

"Wishful thinking?" Callum asked.

Amarande shrugged but otherwise didn't rise to the bait. "Handyman?"

"What of it?"

"I should think you of all people would have thought of a disguise that wouldn't blow your cover."

Callum lifted one brow. "I would have if a cover had been needed."

Disbelief colored his tone. "You expect me to believe that you actually work here?"

Callum folded his ladder and grabbed his bucket. "I don't really give a damn what you believe."

Before Callum could walk away, Amarande stepped in front of him. "Are you monitoring anyone attending the council meetings?"

"Vampire I don't report to you or anyone else in your precious council so you best move out of my space before I step all over you."

That was as good as an answer as he could ever hope to get out of Callum. "Does General Thomson know you're here?"

Without looking back Callum answered, "Probably. But I don't report to him either so it doesn't really matter."

Amarande watched one of the world's most lethal killers walk away.

His first name was all he knew about the man. That and the fact that he had been attached to one of the special forces units. But no one was quite sure which one. The man was pretty much a walking mystery.

Rumors circulated a few years back that Callum had gone underground. He thought perhaps Callum had finally met his match and taken a bullet to the chest. To see him here, healthy as a horse as far as he could tell, was more than a little unsettling.

What would he want with the Vampire Council? Callum said he didn't report to any of them.

He and Callum might not be friends, but Callum was known for being truthful. He was also the kind of guy who didn't mind sharing news when he knew you wouldn't like it.

Even knowing that Tullamore was neutral ground did not make him feel better. Despite the fact that even Callum couldn't violate that rule and get away with it.

Amarande frowned as he went in the opposite direction. There were too many unknowns at work this weekend. It made him more than a little antsy.

"Amarande!" He stopped when he heard Shaia's voice. He didn't even have to pretend to be happy to see her. She was one of the few genuinely welcome faces he had seen all weekend. Perhaps all month. He leaned down to accept and return a kiss on the cheek.

"I had so hoped to see you before dinner." Shaia slipped her arm through his and steered him in the direction she wanted him to go.

"How are you?" he asked.

"Very well. How are you holding up with the trials?"

"Fine." The less said, the better. But he could never hide anything from her.

"Edrigu tells me they are going well. What is your opinion?"

"I think they are going well. I am looking forward to today's physical challenge."

She patted the arm she held. "Of course you are. You have always been a competitor."

In a lower tone he added, "And I received some kind of clue to solve for another of them."

"And?"

"And I'm uncertain what to do with it."

Shaia stopped walking and faced him. "You've never been uncertain of anything in your life. What's going on?"

He glanced left then glared at the man who hovered too close to them on their right. The man hurried away.

Shaia shot Amarande a disapproving look. "Perhaps we should slip in here for this discussion." She gestured to the empty conference room just across the hall from where they stood. When they stepped inside, she told the youngling who was unpacking a box at the head of the conference table, "Would you excuse us for a few moments?"

The youngling's eyes widened in surprise. "Of course." She hurried out the door, pulling it closed behind her.

Shaia patted one of the leather chairs. "Sit." She pulled the chair next to it out. "Tell me what's going on with you." Graceful as always, she sat down and crossed her legs. At a glance, most would never suspect that she was well over five hundred years.

He dutifully did as she asked. One of the few people in the world he respected enough to do so. "The trials have gone well."

"I didn't ask about the trials. I asked about you."

He gave her a placating smile. "I'm well, nire ama." *My Mother.* Since she and Edrigu had taken him in not long after his turning, he'd long considered Shaia his vampire mother.

"It may have been some time since I last saw you, but I can still sense when something is not quite right. When did you last feed?"

He smiled. Sometimes he missed having someone to worry over him. "Before I arrived at Tullamore."

"Hmmm. And when were you last with a woman?"

Shaia had always been direct in her questions but he still had work to keep his face impassive. "Not so long ago."

"Still no one of particular interest then?"

Reaghan's face popped to mind. "No."

One delicately arched brow rose. "I believe that is not quite the truth."

"It's nothing." He answered just a little too fast. "She can be nothing, ama. There is no point getting into it."

The leather crackled as she sat back in her chair. "Tell me about her."

He sighed. He wasn't getting out of this interrogation any time soon unless he told her what she wanted to know. "I just met her."

"Here?"

"Yes." If he wasn't careful, Shaia would track Reaghan down and interrogate her.

Her brow rose. "Interesting."

"But like I said, nothing about it will work." Even though he said the words, he didn't completely buy into them.

"Why not?"

"Because she's human." Then again, so was he, at one point.

"Ah." Shaia nodded her understanding. "That is unfortunate."

"But..." He hesitated saying anything more.

"But?" She prompted.

"But when I first saw her I felt..." He lifted his distressed gaze to meet hers. "I swear I heard the faint echo of my heart beat."

Shaia's normally composed expression faltered and she gasped in surprise. She leaned forward and reached for his hand. "Have you tasted her yet?"

Images of Reaghan's head thrown back, her neck exposed, burrowed into his mind's eye. "No."

"You must." She squeezed his hand. "It's the only way to know for sure if she's your heartmate."

"It won't work, ama. Even if she is the one." There. Cold, hard logic. That was what he needed to survive this bombardment of feelings.

"How do you know that?"

He got up from the chair so he could pace. "She's human."

"So?" Frustration made Shaia's normally calm demeanor slip.

"You know as well as I do what that means. She has a mortal lifespan."

"You could turn her," she suggested.

"That is a big maybe." There hadn't been a successfully turned human in over a hundred years. At least not that they knew of. When humans were unable to survive the turning, they experienced an excruciating death. Very few even risked it anymore.

"If you become a clan leader you will need a good woman beside you. A heartmate would be ideal."

"Yes, a turned heartmate would be ideal, but it could also kill her."

"Are you saying you would rather never know?"

"I'm saying I think I should get through the trials, ascertain how probable a Clan Leader position is, then address personal issues."

"And what if she leaves here and pledges herself to a mortal man in the mean time?"

He growled. "I could argue that it wasn't meant to be and she wasn't really the one."

Her eyes narrowed to slits as she studied him. "I think we both know that's a lie."

His fingers dug into the back of the chair he stopped beside. "If the council learns about this, they could use it against me. I would lose standing in the trials." He held her gaze. "You know that as well as I."

"True." She nodded her agreement.

"I honestly believe the best course of action is to wait until after the trials."

"If you can wait that long to find out, then she isn't the one."

Shaia got up from her chair. "Don't waste your time or hers. Your heartmate won't leave your mind for even a moment once you find her. No matter what else is going on around you. She will haunt you and she will make you whole. Nothing more and nothing less."

He was afraid to breathe.

"I touched a nerve, didn't I?" She sat in her chair again and studied him. "You're afraid."

Amarande couldn't lie to her so it was pointless to deny it, so he said nothing.

"Come." She patted the chair next to her. "I will tell you all the things about heartmates that your kind will not."

He scoffed. "My kind?"

She smirked. "Men, of course."

Amarande frowned as he took the seat next to her.

"Finding a heartmate is a beautifully rare thing. It's something to be treasured. What your kind fails to understand is what that bond means for the woman."

"I should think it means the same as it does for men."

"In many ways, yes, you are correct." She folded her hands together. "Men typically see it as an unbreakable commitment between two souls. Which it is. It transcends any human marriage vows much less a contracted marriage." She held one finger up. "For a woman it goes much deeper. We become our mate's weakness and his strength. When you're talking about powerful leaders like Edrigu." She gestured to Amarande. "Or you. Your enemies would only have to find her if they truly want to take you down."

A cold chill washed over him. Amarande knew what Edrigu would do if someone were to attempt harming Shaia. He felt certain if he found his own heartmate that he would tear down heaven to protect her. "You said she is his strength too."

"Yes. Emotionally and physically."

"I don't mean to doubt what you're saying, but how can she be his physical strength?"

"A heartmate can take her partner's pain, illness, or injury and replace it with her own strength and wholeness."

"She can?" Why had he never heard of this?

"Yes. The price is that she herself becomes injured or ill. It's an exchange. His weakness for her strength."

He blinked at the revelation. He was both fascinated and horrified by the thought.

"As you can well imagine, it is a closely guarded secret. Very few know how to do it and even fewer have actually done it."

He studied her face. "You and Edrigu have though?"

"Once. During the war." She smiled at the memory. "He didn't realize what I was doing at the time. But later, after the heat of battle had faded, he saw what I endured during my recovery. He was quite cross with me and forbid me from ever doing it again."

"I imagine he would."

"My point in all of this is that you need to remember you're not the only one making a commitment. She is too. And she does have a choice. If you act as if she and your commitment to each other are unimportant, she will too. And you could very well lose her. I've seen it happen." She pinned him to his chair with a look. "If she really is your heartmate, and you want her—human or no—you had best secure her or someone else will. Don't be a fool and risk it."

"I will consider all you have said."

"Good. Now…" She got to her feet. "If you aren't too busy for an old lady, you can escort me to the ladies tea."

He stood as soon as she did. "Ama, you will forever be ageless to me." He offered his arm to her. "And I would be delighted to escort you anywhere you would like to go."

She patted his cheek. "You may be our fiercest Enforcer yet, but I still see the vulnerable man beneath that hard exterior." She twined her arm through the one he offered her. "And do bring this young lady around once you've gotten your head on straight. I'd very much like to meet her."

11

A section of the hotel grounds had been blocked off for the physical challenges. Amarande arrived ahead of time in order to inspect the setup. Since he hadn't been able to glean any information from anyone, he hoped seeing the site would help him figure out what the council had in store for them.

He always relished a challenge. Add in a little competition and he was ready to go.

There were tents set up along one side of a large walled in area. A multi-level seating area had been set along the opposite wall.

"Amarande." Willem approached. "I had hoped to speak to you last night but didn't see you come out after your interviews."

The two men clasped forearms in greeting.

"It's good to see you, Willem," Amarande said. "It has been too long."

"Indeed."

The two men continued toward the seating area together. They climbed the steps into the viewing area to get a look over the wall. The arena had been set up with what appeared to be a finish line at one end and a few obstacles placed randomly on the track.

"What do you think they have in mind for us?" Willem asked.

Amarande crossed his arms over his chest. "Fighting. A problem or puzzle to solve."

"I take it you were unable to obtain hints from anyone."

"Nope." Amarande glanced at Willem. "You?"

"Not a word. They're playing this one close to the chest."

"There is a lot at stake."

"For us or them?" Willem asked.

"Good question."

A group of the younger, cockier contestants headed toward the arena entrance. Like a pack of untamed wolves, they pushed and shoved at each other. One of them even jumped on the back of one of the others. Willem curled his lips in distain.

Amarande muttered, "Even our younglings behave better than that."

A line of contestants strolled in not far behind the juveniles.

"How do you think this will turn out?" Willem asked.

"Based on the number of far less experienced candidates in our midst, I expect between you, me, Inigo, Dunixi, and Aksel, we'll push at least eighty percent of the pool to the bottom of the list. There are one or two that I don't know anything about so that percentage may be a little heavy, but I doubt by much."

Willem nodded. "Agreed. The thing I don't understand is why the council didn't narrow the field right off. It certainly would have saved some time and effort."

"I've been wondering the same," Amarande agreed.

"Positive publicity?"

"For whom?" Amarande asked.

Willem shrugged. "Clans would be less likely to send candidates to future trials if theirs were turned down for this one."

"Perhaps." Despite their willingness to come together to face outside threats, the clans tended to be rather cut-throat when it came to internal conflicts.

A youngling wearing a black and red striped shirt approached them from inside the ring. "Gentlemen, I believe they are ready to give a briefing to all candidates. Would you mind terribly joining the rest of the group under the large white tent?"

Willem and Amarande exchanged long suffering glances. "Of course," Amarande told the youngling.

As they headed to the tent, Willem told him, "Before we get any further in the competition, I wanted to wish you good luck."

Amarande briefly clasped Willem on the shoulder. "Same to you, my friend."

"I'll do my best to not damage anything vital today," Willem told him with a mischievous grin.

"And I suppose you expect me to return the favor?" Amarande smirked back.

"It would be the gentleman thing to do."

"Would it?" Amarande scoffed. "Aren't you the one who said I sucked at being a gentleman?"

"Did I say that?"

"I am pretty sure that was you."

"Doesn't sound like me."

"Hmmm."

When they reached the back of the group of contestants they fell silent.

They listened while the event coordinator gave them an overview of the event. The first half would be series of races and one-on-one matches. Those made it through would move into a final event and face an un-named beast, en masse.

Willem and Amarande exchanged puzzled glances. The council had outlawed the use of animals for events where the beast was likely to be injured for sport about fifty years prior.

"Just so you know," the coordinator told them. "The beast will be no ordinary animal. It will be one conjured specifically by Mage Roberto." He held up one finger. "Now before you start thinking it will be easy to defeat, please understand that this beast will have the power to draw blood and crush your bones." He waited until he had the entire group's attention to continue. "We cannot stress enough that it is entirely possible for you to die in this competition." He paused for effect. "Does anyone have questions?"

He answered the few the other attendees asked then directed them to a tent where they could prepare for the event.

They were allowed to select from a variety of protection gear. Some of the younger ones grabbed heavy armor and helmets that restricted your vision unnecessarily. Without knowing what they were facing, Amarande kept his gear simple. A couple of leather arm protectors suited him well enough. After all, he was used to fighting with nothing more than whatever he was wearing at the time.

Weapons, however, were forbidden for the first series.

The candidates were divided into four groups. Then names were called to enter the ring.

The first couple of events were foot races and with a small obstacle course. Of course they were racing a challenger. Along the way it became clear that it wasn't enough to beat your opponent on speed. It was about out-maneuvering them as well.

Amarande easily won his first two. Willem did as well. A few of the younger cocky contestants were eliminated.

The next events became more challenging. Not only did they

have to overcome much larger obstacles, but they also needed to be able to defend themselves from the natural threats interwoven into the course as well as their opponents.

Amarande disarmed his opponent before making it halfway through the third course. But his fourth race took a little more effort. As he worked to knock his opponent out of the race he kept reminding himself to do so without doing permanent harm.

Unlike some of the younger candidates, he had nothing to prove by killing an opponent. Likewise, he gained nothing by seriously harming them. He simply needed to ensure they remained out of his way.

Toward the end of his third event he spotted Reaghan in the stands. His eye was automatically drawn to her pale hair.

It very nearly cost him secure footing as he crossed a particularly difficult section. Now that he knew she was watching, he had another reason to want to do well.

At the end of the first half, the top contestants were himself, Willem, two others Amarande knew and a half dozen younger vamps he didn't know. They were allowed to retreat to the equipment tent for a short rest while they prepared the arena for the second half.

After selecting his weapons and donning a thin chainmail shirt, Amarande went in search of refreshment.

"Hey Amarande." One of the younger vamps descended on him along with two of his cronies. "Rodolf said you cheated during your match." He puffed up his chest, trying to looking intimidating. "I'm calling you out on that."

The room went silent.

"What did you just say?" Amarande asked with deadly calm.

"You heard me." He closed in on Amarande. "You cheated. And I'm here to set it right."

"You have five seconds to step out of my space before I end your brief appearance in this competition."

"Gentlemen." Lord Edrom called out as he entered the tent. "I believe you would do well to save that aggression for the field."

Amarande's gaze never wavered from the younger vampire. One of the younger vampire's friends pulled him to the other side of the room.

"I wish to congratulate you on making it this far in the competition," Lord Edrom continued as if the incident had never occurred. "We're excited to see what Mage Roberto has dreamed up for you. And even more to see how each of you fare." He tapped his cane on the ground. "Now, I wish you all good luck and we'll see a few of you in the winner's circle."

Lord Edrom and Gaspard, Lord Edrom's son, made their way around the room, saying a few words to each of the contestants. When they reached Amarande, Lord Edrom shook his hand and mumbled some unimportant greeting about how well he was doing. Throughout Lord Edrom's meet and greet he felt someone staring at him. Sure enough, when he checked for the source, he found the hostile young vampire glaring at him.

By the time Lord Edrom finished talking with everyone, Amarande was more than ready to get on with the last event. He had a clue to solve, a potential heartmate to figure out, a council to impress, and apparently a young vamp to teach a lesson to.

After Lord Edrom left one of the event coordinators called out names and directed each of them where to go. Once everyone had lined up in the appropriate areas, the event began. Contestants spilled onto the field to face their opponents.

Amarande focused on disarming his opponent immediately to ensure completing the course went quickly. By the time they finished all of the rounds, it had come down to the group he expected from the start. The one unknown was the angry young vamp who had tried to pick a fight with him earlier in the evening.

His gut told him that the young vamp's ire was not due to an allegation of cheating. Especially given the safeguards the council put in place to prevent cheating. But it would take more time than he had to figure it out. Perhaps it would be better for everyone if he eliminated that vamp from the competition and moved on.

Back in the contestant's tent, Amarande grabbed a bottle of water and guzzled half of it down. He left the bottle on a table while he retrieved one of the lightweight chest protectors. Once he had it in place he tested his maneuverability, made adjustments where needed, then armed himself. He opted for multiple small knives and one short sword. Guns were forbidden in the event as was the use of silver which only made him long for weapons from his personal inventory. But his training, however, ensured he could work with any weapon. He was also capable of turning simple, everyday items into something lethal.

When he finished his preparations, he returned to his place next to the sofa. He reached for the bottle of water he had left but Willem cautioned him, "I don't recommend drinking that."

Amarande glanced at Willem then realization dawned. He lifted the open bottle to his nose and sniffed the contents. Sure enough he detected a faint chemical odor. He frowned. He wasn't certain, but he thought it smelled like sativornix. While not deadly, it made vampires quite ill if consumed. Everything from dizziness to stomach cramping. Definitely not what you'd want to succumb to during battle.

He and Willem searched the group for the angry young vamp.

The vamp in question, of course, was making no attempt to mask his loathing for Amarande.

"How do you suppose he managed to smuggle in sativornix? They checked everyone for weapons."

"No telling, but I have to give him credit for having the balls to do it."

Amarande nodded.

"My question is why does he seem fixated on you?"

"He said I cheated when I bested one of his friends."

Willem snorted. "Right. I'd say there was more to it than that."

"So would I, but it doesn't look as if I'll have enough time to figure it out." Amarande tipped his head toward the tent entrance where the event coordinator had returned. "I think our break time is up."

"Guess you'll have to settle it on the field." Willem clasped Amarande on the shoulder. "Watch your back, my friend."

"Thanks. See you at the finish line."

Willem grinned. "I'll be waiting for you."

Amarande chuckled.

12

REAGHAN fidgeted in her seat as the participants raced onto the playing field. Right away she spotted Amarande, but then she lost sight of him as he ducked behind one of the many obstacles. The first few competitions had been mildly entertaining. They were mostly foot races and competitions that demonstrated the candidates' strength, balance, and wit. They rapidly became more challenging and dangerous as the event moved along. More than one participant had to be carried off the field.

Amarande, however, had done quite well. He was obviously in excellent shape. She thought his suit pants fit him well the first time she saw him. They were nothing compared to the skin-tight body suit he wore now. A pair of looking glasses would have been helpful to get a closer view. It was a shame she was unable to conjure a pair.

She should probably feel guilty for ogling him, but since this was a competition of bachelors on the hunt for potential brides she didn't.

During the break, when the field was prepared for the last part of the competition, she finally spotted Eirin in the stands not far from her. She rushed over to that section of the stands hoping to catch her. When she reached the right one, she spotted a guard posted at the entrance. He turned away the couple who tried to enter just ahead of her telling them that it was a reserved section. Only those invited by Lord Greenwood were allowed to entrance.

Even though she was disappointed she couldn't talk with Eirin, Reaghan was relieved to confirm she was at least at Tullamore. Surely there would be an opportunity for her to talk to Eirin directly later that night, at the dinner.

She returned to the section she had been sitting in. There weren't assigned seats, but since her view of the field was so good, she didn't want to lose it. Besides, from there she could also observe Eirin without alerting her. When she returned to her seat, she realized there were far more spectators. As a distraction until the games started once more, she chatted with the young lady who came and sat next to her.

She learned that the young lady had opted to not participate in the games but still hoped to meet some of the bachelors to determine if they might suit.

Reaghan's gut clenched knowing Amarande was one of the potential bachelors. She almost asked the girl about him, but bit her tongue. After all, this wasn't her world. She would be leaving soon to return to hers.

As discreetly as possible, she kept one eye on Eirin. Eirin smiled and laughed as if she didn't have a care in the world. The young man she sat with was quite attentive to her. He seemed to go out of his way to make her laugh. Even when he was drawn into conversation with others, he held her hand or touched her in some way. From everything she could tell, this was a young couple who were very much into each other. She saw nothing to cause her alarm or make her think that Eirin was being held against her will.

She still needed to hear the proof of it from Eirin herself. But she would make sure to convey her observations to the queen as well as Eirin's father.

Trumpets blared signaling the start of the last event. The remaining participants ran out onto the track and readied themselves. Once again Reaghan had no problem spotting Amarande. This time she would have sworn he looked right at her. Her blood stirred in response.

Three blasts from a horn started the race.

For a moment she thought it would also be a simple foot race, but as the group moved toward the goal, the ground began to tremble. Crystal shaped rocks shot upward from the ground forming a barrier between the starting line and the finish. At least one participant had the misfortune of standing in the exact spot where a rock erupted. The force was enough to toss him over the wall of the arena and toward the crowd. That candidate suddenly stopped mid-flight and remained suspended just above the arena wall as if he had been stuck to an invisible barrier.

Whoever organized the event must have help from someone with magical abilities. Under normal circumstances, she would stop to find out who, but that wasn't part of her mission. It might however be prudent to avoid that person, just in case.

The participants, now aware of the danger, pressed onward toward the goal with more caution. Amarande lingered somewhere in the middle of the pack.

As they climbed over and through the new obstacles, they also wrestled and fought each other. Every time someone drew close to Amarande she had to resist the urge to shout a warning to him. Not that he would have heard her over the roar of the crowd.

More than once Amarande had to fight one of the other men. She winced every time he took a hit. But unless she was very much mistaken, he only fought to defend himself and even then he only incapacitated his opponent. Unlike a couple of the other participants who seemed to try to inflict as much damage as possible.

One opponent in particular went for Amarande more than once, making her wonder if there was something personal about his attacks. After the last bout words were very obviously exchanged. Amarande handled himself well and merely rendered his opponent unconscious. At least that was how it appeared.

A bone-rattling squawk from overhead made her and most of the crowd jump. An over-sized bird-like creature swooped into the arena drawing gasps from the onlookers. The candidates closest to the bird's landing spot scrambled to get away from the creature's talons as they sank into the dirt and grass.

The bird swiveled its head left and right, as if tracking the movement of those around him. Using its long beak as a weapon, it pecked at any candidate within stabbing distance.

The crowd gasped when one of the candidates fell and couldn't get away fast enough. Even from her seat Reaghan could see blood soaking the ground where he held his leg. Reaghan held her breath. There was no way he'd be able to get away from that bird with an injury like that.

In a blur, Amarande and one other participant sprinted to the downed man. Amarande grabbed the man under the arm and pulled him away while the other participant did what he could to distract the bird.

Reaghan clutched at the edge of her sweater until she saw Amarande emerge from the shadows of the structure where he had taken the injured player. Only then did she breathe a sigh of relief.

Amarande and the participant who distracted the bird met up and charged toward the objective. Based on how well they worked together to evade the bird and the other obstacles, she wondered if they knew each other.

With only a few more close calls, Amarande and two others reached the goal at the same time. All three of them laughed when the prize – a gaudy child size trophy – was revealed. The crowd erupted in even louder applause and cheers when the younger of the three raised it in victory.

She watched the round of congratulations for a moment, then hurried out of the stands in hopes of catching Eirin as she left. She managed to spot the group Eirin was with over the crowd, but couldn't catch up to them. While frustrated that she couldn't complete her mission then and there, it was probably for the best. Tracking Eirin down in from of a crowd of vampires would likely draw more attention than she wanted. Instead, she asked one of the event personnel where she might find the participants. He directed her to a large white tent stationed at one side of the arena. He also cautioned her that no one was allowed in and that her best chance would be when they made the walk back to the hotel afterward.

Reaghan found a bench situated next to the walkway and waited for Amarande. As she waited, she pondered why she felt compelled to speak with him despite knowing the reason for him competing in the event.

Her attraction to him made no sense at all. But she could not deny it. Oddly, she sensed some sort of connection to him. Those brief moments when they touched only compounded it. And so, here she was, waiting for a man – no, a vampire – just because she needed to make sure he was all right.

When she finally spotted him heading her way, her heart skipped a beat. At the same moment he looked up. She was too far away to clearly see his express but his gait faltered when he saw her. She hoped that she had surprised him in a good way.

"Congratulations on winning," she said when he finally reached her.

"Thank you."

For once in her life, she didn't know what to say to a man. Yet she craved conversation with him so she blurted out the first thing she could think of as they walked toward the hotel. "It appeared to be a three-way tie. Is that right?"

He shrugged. "Depends on how the council wishes to tell the story."

"Was that the end of the trials then?" It was probably too much to hope for, but she asked anyway.

"No."

"So…" She grimaced. "Will the other events be like that one?"

He chuckled. "No."

"Good." Her gaze drifted over him, landing on a bandage he had wrapped just above one of his writs. "How are you?"

"I'm fine." He made a fist and held up the injured arm. "We heal quickly."

"Still, that was a rather brutal event. Is there anyone you can see about your injury?"

"Yes, if I needed a healer we have one. But I'm fine, really." He shrugged. "I suppose it would seem brutal if you aren't used to this sort of thing."

"Are there people used to this?" It was foolish to think so, but she hoped no one had to live such a harsh life.

"Unfortunately." His expression blanked as if he didn't want her to see what he was thinking about. Memories, perhaps?

"Like you?"

He shrugged again and opened the door to the hotel for her.

His lack of answer spoke volumes. But it also cautioned her that she truly didn't know this man and she would do well to tread carefully where he was concerned. "So now what?" she asked.

"Now I shower, change clothes, and wait for dinner."

She nodded. It sounded simple, but after a day of fighting men and a magical beast, he had to be tired. "Are you going to be up to singing tonight?"

"Of course." His answer implied she was being silly to think otherwise.

"Well, I suppose you didn't have to strain your voice, right?"

Finally, he gave her a glimmer of a smile. "Thankfully no."

At a loss as to what else to say to him she lamely asked, "Then, I guess I'll see you at dinner?"

"You most certainly will." His voice dropped to a lower, more intimate tone.

Once again it felt as if a wave a warmth washed through her body when their eyes met.

They remained locked in each other's gaze until someone walked up to offer their congratulations to Amarande. She used the opportunity to quietly escape to her room before she did something foolish, like offering to let him join her.

It was for the best, she reminded herself.

Her heart, however, did not agree.

13

REAGHAN headed to the ballroom early in hopes of searching for Eirin as guests filtered in.

The small voice in the back of her mind whispered that Eirin wasn't the only one she would be looking for that evening. She ruthlessly pushed that voice aside.

When she reached the ballroom where the dinner would be held, she was asked to wait for Noémie before entering since her name had not been included on the guest list.

It was good that the event planners were cautious about security. Based on everything she had observed, if she wanted to cause trouble between vampires and the fae, this would be a good time and place to do it. Perhaps that was one of the reasons Caoilfhinn didn't trust anyone else for this mission.

Despite what she had experienced when she was attacked, she had been able to come to terms with it being the actions of one lone vampire. One who wrongfully believed he was above reproach. The whole species was not to blame for his errant thinking.

Things could escalate quickly if she made a mistake while at the meeting. However, things would go far worse if she didn't get the information her queen needed. She swallowed the bubble of fear that pressed at her chest and focused on what she could control at that moment.

Noémie soon joined her. "I'm so sorry you had to wait. I've been going non-stop since the trials earlier today and failed to add your name to the guest list."

Reaghan waved her concern away. "It really was no bother."

"Your dress is gorgeous. I love it," Noémie gushed.

"Thank you." She ran her hand down the petal soft wisps of

fabric that fluttered about her waist. "A friend of mine made it."

"You'll have to pass their name along. They do beautiful work."

Reaghan crinkled her nose. "I'm afraid she doesn't sew professionally. She makes most of her own clothes. This one she made as a gift to accommodate the dancing I do with my routines. I will pass your compliment along though. I've told her many times that she missed her true calling." She stuck as close to the truth as possible since many vampires were able to detect a lie. Caoilfhinn had created her dress, but instead of a sewing machine she used magic.

"I would agree." Noémie pulled her clipboard to her chest. "Is there anything you need before tonight's performance?"

"Not that I can think of." Reaghan glanced about the room. "I assume the schedule remains unchanged? That I am to play after dinner then again after dessert and the speeches?"

"Yes." Noémie consulted her clipboard. "We seated you at one of the tables near the stage. You'll be one table away from Lord Edrom and his family. But we thought it would make it easier for you to access the stage."

"Thank you. That will do very well." She truly couldn't complain about how well she had been treated by everyone at the event. A nagging voice in the back of her mind wondered if that would still be true if they knew she was fae.

"Would you like for me to place your violin on the stage for you?"

"I suppose that would be best." Reaghan reluctantly handed Noémie the case.

"I will ask one of our security guards to keep an eye on it for you."

"Thank you." That extra effort made Reaghan feel a little better about letting go of her violin.

"Name tents have been used at the tables at the front of the room but the remainder of the room is open seating." Noémie gestured toward the open doors of the adjoining room. "As you can probably tell, the bar is open if you wish to partake. Hors d'oeuvres have been stationed around the room."

"Do you know who I will be sitting with for dinner?" She crossed her fingers hoping to hear the name of one particular vampire.

"I believe Lord and Lady Bettingham, from one of our English clans and Lord Nakamura and his wife, from our clan in Japan. Oh and Lord Edrom's son, Gaspard. We left the other two seats open in case Gaspard needed them."

Reaghan nodded, disappointed that Amarande would not be sitting with her, even though she knew it had been a distant possibility.

"If there is anything you need this evening, please be sure to let me know."

"Thank you, I will." The younger woman hurried away with the violin leaving Reaghan to enter the reception area on her own. As usual for large gatherings, most people had crowded close to the bar but there were a few clusters dotted around the room. Most likely near the stations of food.

She scanned the crowd looking for Eirin's light colored hair. Unfortunately, there were several ladies fitting that description. Without magic to assist her, she would have to get closer to know for sure if it was Eirin.

"Ah, Mademoiselle McCarthy."

Reaghan turned at the sound of Lord Edrom's voice. "Good evening, Lord Edrom." She plastered her best diplomatic smile on. The two ladies that accompanied him were stunningly beautiful women with similar features. One appeared slightly older leading Reaghan to guess they were mother and daughter. Or at least close relations.

"I'm glad you arrived early. My wife has been most anxious to meet you." Lord Edrom's eyes softened when he looked at the woman whose hand rested on his left arm. "This, my dear, is Mademoiselle McCarthy."

The woman's face brightened and she rushed forward to grasp Reaghan's hand. "I'm so excited to meet you. When Noémie told us she had been able to talk you into coming at the last minute, it made my weekend."

"Thank you, so much. It's nice to meet you too." There weren't that many recordings of her music so it always surprised her when people remarked that they loved it. "I'm glad my schedule allowed me to come. Tullamore is a beautiful property. Whoever booked it chose well."

"Oh I couldn't agree more." Lady Edrom practically beamed positivity and light where as her husband had a darker, domineering presence. "Tullamore is a wonderful place. Our gatherings have been held here for years. We always look forward to them."

Lord Edrom added, "Mademoiselle McCarthy I'd also like to introduce you to our daughter, Kesila."

Reaghan bolstered her smile and shook the other woman's hand. Kesila had a surprisingly firm grip for someone who looked as if she had just stepped out of a designer fashion show. Her hair had been styled so that it flowed over one shoulder like a cascade of jet black silk. It made a stunning contrast against her pale skin and crimson colored gown. "It's lovely to meet you. Mother raved so much about your music that I am anxious to hear you play."

Reaghan had never been self-conscious before, but standing near Kesila, she felt a touch underdressed. Odd, since her objective was to blend in, not stand out. "Hopefully I'll have something that appeals to you as well."

"There you all are." A handsome young man wearing an impeccably tailored suit strolled up to their group. "Sorry to be late."

"Gaspard, come and meet Mademoiselle McCarthy." Lady Edrom extended her hand.

The young man's dark hair and hazel eyes were almost identical to Lord Edrom's. Even the shape of their chins was similar. Reaghan knew he must be some relation as well.

Gaspard made no effort to hide his assessment of her figure as he reached for her hand. "It's a pleasure to meet you, Mademoiselle McCarthy. Will you be joining us for dinner tonight, then?"

An airy chuckle came from Kesila. "She's the human entertainer tonight, brother. Did you not hear Mother telling us about her over luncheon?"

Kesila's emphasis on the word human touched one of Reaghan's nerves. Despite the fact that she wasn't actually human. But the way Kesila said it hinted that she had little respect for that race.

"Indeed?" Gaspard's next visual appraisal said Reaghan had lost some value in his eyes. Not that she truly cared. "I have more than one business deal in the works that are taking up a considerable amount of my thoughts. I must have missed that."

"Oh, Gaspard," Lady Edrom chided. "You and your father work far too hard."

"There is much to do in a limited time." He shot a meaningful glance at his father. "We wouldn't be nearly so busy if we could have these gatherings more than once a decade."

"No business talk tonight," Lord Edrom reminded him. He smiled at Reaghan. "Tonight is about renewing old friendships and making new ones."

"A delightful notion," Reaghan agreed.

"Mademoiselle McCarthy, since it seems that we are both without dining partners, I would be happy to escort you in," Gaspard said.

While his offer was made with every courtesy, she could tell from his bored expression that he didn't really want to. "Thank you. I—"

"That won't be necessary, Gaspard." Reaghan's heart turned flips when Amarande interrupted. "I'll be escorting her in." His tone, while polite, brooked no argument.

Reaghan was so surprised by his declaration that she almost missed Kesila's reaction. The young woman must have had her own intentions for Amarande since her surprise turned to ire then back to well-rehearsed indifference in a matter of seconds.

"Ah, Amarande. I wondered where you were." Lord Edrom closed the distance between them and shook hands with him. "I assume you two have everything worked out?" He cast a meaningful glance at Reaghan.

"Yes, I believe we have," Amarande looked down at her for confirmation.

Reaghan cleared the lump from her throat. "Yes, of course."

Lord Edrom gave a quick nod. "Good."

"Do they have what worked out, father?" Kesila asked.

"Nothing you need to worry about." Lord Edrom smiled as he dismissed his daughter's question outright. "Come, my dear." He took his wife's hand and replaced it on his arm. "We have other guests we are neglecting."

Lady Edrom smiled at each of them in the group. "Enjoy your evening."

"I suppose I should make my rounds as well." Gaspard gave Amarande a brisk nod then followed his father into the crowd.

Kesila had stalled, as if waiting to say something but Lady Edrom prevented it. "Kesila, Lady Camilia is hovering near the Van Hassenburgs. Perhaps you should go say hello."

"Of course, Mother." Kesila shot Amarande a look that hinted at some connection between the two.

Even though she had no claim on Amarande's time or affection, something about Kesila's behavior toward him rubbed Reaghan the wrong way.

"You look beautiful," Amarande told Reaghan after everyone had walked away.

The intimate tone he used washed through her like a caress. "Thank you." She gestured to him. "You are certainly doing that tuxedo justice."

"You think so?"

"I do." What was she doing flirting with a vampire? Had she lost her ever loving mind? But then again, he was a handsome devil. And the tuxedo only intensified that. Not that she had seen him wear anything except black so far.

"I'm glad you like it." He offered his arm to her. "Shall we mingle?"

"I suppose it is the thing to do, isn't it?" She wrapped her hand around his arm and forced herself to ignore the flash of awareness touching him always brought.

"Unfortunately." His tone said he could do without the social interaction. Normally she could as well, but she needed to find Eirin. And tonight was her best opportunity.

Amarande led Reaghan through a circuit around the perimeter of the room. Neither of them felt the need for unnecessary chit-chat, but occasionally she asked him for name of people just to have some back and forth conversation. Most especially those she had spotted earlier at the competition, sitting in the same area as Eirin.

It seemed he knew most everyone there but he rarely stopped to speak with anyone. Several people avoided making eye contact with him and a couple even hurried away when they saw him approach. The few who did voluntarily speak with him didn't seem to know him on a personal level.

Was it because of him or the fact that he escorted what they all thought was a human?

He had said he was an enforcer of vampire law. It was possible he had history with the people they encountered. She was still pondering whether the reactions were based in fear or respect when Amarande groaned then whispered in her ear, "I'm sorry for what is about to happen."

"What—" Reaghan's question was cut off by a woman's declaration.

"Amarande, dear boy. There you are." A path parted in the crowd revealing a strikingly beautiful older woman being escorted by a suave, silver haired gentleman.

The woman leaned toward Amarande obviously expecting a kiss on the cheek. Amarande obliged her with a tender smile.

Reaghan couldn't decide if she was more surprised by the familiarity or the obvious affection the three had for each other. Perhaps they were family?

They woman glanced at Reaghan. "I would ask what you were doing here this early, but I believe I know the answer."

Amarande ignored her comment and went right to the introductions. "Lord and Lady Moreschi, this is Miss Reaghan McCarthy. She is the guest violinist tonight."

"It's lovely to meet you." Lady Moreschi clasped hands with Reaghan. The woman's expression briefly faltered as she looked deep into Reaghan's eyes. For a moment Reaghan feared she had seen past her glamour. But then Lady Moreschi's smile returned and Reaghan wondered if she had just imagined it.

Lord Moreschi bowed over her hand. "Anyone who has the power to bring this one out of his lair before the main course hits the table must be talented indeed."

She glanced at Amarande in question. "I wasn't aware that I had anything to do with his being here at all." Why would they think such a thing?

"Edrigu is giving me a hard time, not you." Amarande shot a pointed look at Lord Moreschi. "You should be grateful I'm here at all. You know how much I hate attending these things."

Lord Moreschi chuckled. "I do. Why do you think I've always insisted you attend?"

"So you play the violin?" Lady Moreschi asked. "I have always enjoyed the stringed instruments. I don't suppose you like to play any of the classical masters, do you? I'm afraid I don't listen to very much modern music."

"Actually, I am classically trained but I play a variety of songs. Everything from classical Baroque to modern pop and even jazz."

"That's wonderful!" Lady Moreschi looked up at her husband. "I do wish that Terese has pursued her music lessons. I still believe she would have done well if she had applied herself."

"Terese hated those lessons," Amarande reminded them.

Reaghan hoped that Terese was family and not a former love interest of Amarande's. Not that it should matter.

"She did." Lord Moreschi nodded in agreement. "But you didn't seem to mind them," he added thoughtfully.

"They weren't so bad," Amarande admitted.

Lord Moreschi leaned closer and whispered, "Lord Edrom

80

hinted that you may be assisting with the entertainment tonight. Is this true?"

Amarande shrugged a shoulder without answering.

At that moment the doors to the dining room swung open and one of the hotel staff announced, "Dinner is served."

Amarande grinned. "Guess you'll have to wait and see."

14

THE more time he spent with Reaghan, the more he suspected that Shaia was right. The rapidly accumulating hints indicated Reaghan was indeed his heartmate. It made him anxious to claim her.

But after spending so many years as an Enforcer, he knew nothing about romancing a woman. Much less winning her heart. He had never been so inclined. The life of an Enforcer never allowed for romantic relationships, yet women were never in short supply. They seemed to be drawn to Enforcers. Human and vampire alike.

Something he never understood, yet didn't argue with. After all, sex was almost as important as blood to a vampire.

He kept a close watch on Reaghan through dinner. Would she be a good mate for a clan leader? Assuming everything went the way he hoped, it could be important. She interacted with those at their table with quiet grace. And she was polite, almost kind, to those serving the food.

But the thing that drew him in was the fact, consciously or not, she remained connected with him throughout dinner. Sometimes it was a subtle as a brush of her knee against his under the table. Other times it was a shared glance while she laughed at something someone at the table had said. But most convincing were the times she reached for his hand to catch his attention instead of simply calling his name.

While he couldn't recall what they had for dinner, he had never enjoyed a meal more.

He was surprisingly disappointed when Noémie came to the table to whisper in Reaghan's ear. "Lord Edrom said they were just about ready for you."

"Did he say how long they needed me to play for this first set?" Reaghan asked.

"Only fifteen to twenty minutes while they clear the dinner dishes and serve dessert."

"And my case?"

Noémie pointed to a chair that had been left near the elevated stage.

Reaghan nodded her understanding then Noémie headed to the stage.

Reaghan leaned close to Amarande. "Will you be joining me for this first set? Or would you prefer to wait until later?"

"Now is as good a time as any."

She smiled. "So it is."

Lord Edrom crossed the wood dancefloor and took the microphone from Noémie as the background music faded to silence. "Good evening. I hope everyone has enjoyed their dinner."

There were murmurs of approval through the room.

"We have a special treat for you this evening. Mademoiselle McCarthy, one of the world's finest violinists, is here with us for a rare performance. She has graciously agreed to play while dessert is being served. Then after dinner she will join the house band and play off and on through the evening."

Reaghan stood for the round of polite applause then went to retrieve her violin. Other than a slight tremor in her hand when she brushed a stray lock of hair from her face, she hid any nervousness she might have been feeling.

If they were heartmates he would have reassured her through their connection. The fact that the idea even occurred to him hinted at his rapidly growing attachment.

"Mademoiselle McCarthy, if you will." Lord Edrom gestured for her to take center stage then handed the microphone back to Noémie.

Reaghan dipped into a pseudo-curtsy then placed the violin to her shoulder. She reminded him of a mischievous imp when she grinned and plucked a few notes from the strings. Seemingly satisfied by what she heard, she placed the bow on her instrument and the music flowed. She played a peppy, happy piece he had heard before but one he didn't know the words to.

As was his habit, he checked the room, this time not just for potential threats but to gauge how well the audience liked her playing. He found varying states of reception in the faces he scanned. Some were indifferent, but more than he expected appeared intrigued. By the time the song ended, even a few of the older, more solemn attendees were tapping their fingers or swaying ever so slightly to the music.

Impressive.

She walked to the edge of the dance floor as she transitioned into the second song. The song's tempo sped up and she danced along the edge of the wooden barrier as if entreating those at the tables to join her. Some of her movements reminded him of a graceful ballerina. How did she manage those steps and spins without missing a note or slide of the bow?

The music flowed around the room like magic. By the time the song ended he realized he had forgotten to move to the side of the stage as he originally intended. The crowd applauded.

As she bowed to the audience, she tossed him a questioning glance. He nodded once to reassure her that he still planned to join in. Her smile brightened.

"I believe we have time for one more song before our dessert is served." She announced as she made a couple of adjustments to her instrument. "Those of you who have spent much time here in Ireland may recognize this next one." She stroked the bow across the strings and the first notes blossomed.

He let her play through the repeating verse of the song before he got to his feet and added his voice to the song.

A hush fell across the room. Even the occasional clatter of dishes being stacked at the back of the room stopped.

He sang the next lines as he slowly made his way around the table and met her at the edge of the dance floor. She swayed and twirled around him as he belted out the remaining stanzas. When he finished the last line she came to stand next to him and added an extra flourish at the end of the song. She held his gaze as she let the final notes fade out.

Their connection was electric. It took every ounce of control he possessed to not pull her into his arms right there.

The room burst into thundering applause drawing their attention away from each other. When he looked out at the crowd he found many had risen to their feet. She reached for his hand then gracefully dipped into a dancer's bow.

Lord Edrom was the first to meet them at the stage. "Marvelous. Absolutely marvelous." He shook Amarande's hand then looked at Reaghan. He wore the biggest smile Amarande had ever seen on the elder vampire. "Bravo."

Lady Edrom was right on his heels with her congratulations. She broke with propriety and embraced Reaghan. "That was splendid." She squeezed Amarande's hand. "And you are full of surprises."

He was saved from responding to Lady Edrom's comment by the approach of the next well-wishers. He and Reaghan fielded questions side by side until Lord Edrom announced that dessert had been served.

Amarande took Reaghan's hand and escorted her to the stage so she could return her violin to its case, then on to their table. Even in the dim lighting he could tell her cheeks were flushed.

"Can I get you a drink?" he asked as he pushed her chair in for her.

"Just water for me." She took a long drink from her recently filled glass. "But don't let me stop you if you'd like something more."

"I believe I will follow your lead." He took a drink from his own glass. "For now," he added in a much lower voice.

The widening of her eyes gave away that she had heard him.

As they ate dessert, the house band quietly set up their equipment on stage. The rest of the evening flew by in series of songs, dances, and visits from members of the council. He couldn't be certain where they were going with their questions, but he suspected more than one of them were trying to ascertain if he had his eye on any of the available bachelorettes. Since he had no answer to give them he deftly sidestepped their inquiries.

Late into the evening Reaghan talked him into joining her for two more songs. By then half of the crowd had left to pursue other nightly pleasures so he didn't mind accommodating her.

More than once he caught her scanning the crowd as if looking for someone. But when he confronted her about it she chalked it up to simple curiosity. His instincts said it wasn't quite a lie, nor was it the whole truth. What else it could be evaded him, so he dropped the subject.

After the band and Reaghan gave their final bows, he waited for her to pack her violin and say good night to the band.

Instead of exhausted, she appeared to be energized by her performance. Still, he offered to carry her case for her. He was surprised when she let him.

"How do you think it went?" she asked as soon as they left the ballroom.

"Quite well."

Her smile very nearly took his breath away. "I did too. I haven't played like that in a long time. It felt good to just play without any structure or rules." She practically skipped down the hall. "And the band was great to work with. Their cues were easy to read and we had very similar tastes in music." She spun in a circle. "I don't know why I was so worried about tonight."

"If you were worried, you did a good job hiding it."

Another smile beamed up at him. "Good. I don't usually get nervous but for some reason right before I went up I got a little jittery."

"I doubt anyone noticed." He had. But he had been watching closely. Not that he would admit to it.

They chatted about the things they observed as they made their way to the lobby. When they reached the grand staircase, Kesila intercepted them.

"Amarande." She practically purred his name. "I've been looking for you for hours. I thought for sure you would have found your way to The Dungeon Bar long before now." She ran one perfectly manicured finger across his lapel.

Irritation bubbled in his chest where Kesila had touched him. He wasn't sure all of that irritation belonged to him. He cast a quick glance at Reaghan. A frown now replaced her jubilance.

What was Kesila doing here? Surely there were other men for her to ply her attention upon this evening.

"The band just left the ballroom," Amarande told Kesila as he put a little distance between them. "But I would have thought you knew that."

"Perhaps." She dismissed his comment with a wave of her hand and closed the gap he had created. "As I said, I was looking for you."

"I'll just be going now." Reaghan tugged at the violin case.

Amarande kept his hold on the handle. "I've got it."

"You've got something all right," Reaghan muttered as she tugged on the case again. Still he refused to let go.

Her frown deepened and she held out her hand. "My case, please."

"Kesila, I'm not sure what this is about." He used his free hand to separate himself from Kesila while preventing Reaghan from taking her case. "But I was in the process of escorting Reaghan to her room."

Kesila pressed forward again, blinking her eyes in false innocence. "Does the little human need to be protected from something?"

"No, actually, I—"

Amarande didn't let Reaghan finish her sentence. He checked his temper despite the subtle insult to Reaghan. His instinct was to knock Kesila down several pegs, but as the daughter of the eldest vampire on the council, it might damage his standing. Still, he couldn't let it slide. "I don't know if you have had too much to drink or not quite enough, Kesila. Either way, I suggest you take yourself back to the bar or your room." He growled, "Immediately."

Kesila cast one last hateful glare at Reaghan. "I see. Well…I'm sure Morgen wouldn't mind keeping me company." She turned on her glittery heels and sauntered away.

"Great." Reaghan stomped up the staircase. "Now the daughter of the people who hired me hates me."

Amarande rushed to catch up to her.

"They will probably lose my check." Reaghan muttered. "Assuming they bother to pay me at all."

"Lord Edrom will pay you. He is an honorable man."

"How do I know Miss Prissy Pants there isn't going to run tell her mommy and daddy that I was rude to her or something ridiculous like that?"

"Because I was there to witness it. If anyone was rude to her it was me."

"That's true, but I doubt they'll do or say anything to you." She stopped suddenly and faced him. "Am I right?"

"Most likely."

She bobbed her head once. "Thought as much." She climbed the last few steps to the main floor the turned toward the lobby.

"Are you angry with me?"

"Yes." She grimaced. "No." She huffed and waved his question away. "I don't know. Maybe."

How did she not know whether or not she was angry? "May I ask what I did to anger you?"

"Nothing."

"Then I'm confused."

"So am I. Just forget it." She pressed the button to call the lift.

"It might be easy to forget something that I don't know I've done, but I would prefer to learn from my mistakes."

She sighed. "It wasn't you."

The doors to the lift opened and they stepped inside.

"Was it Kesila?"

"Yes," she growled.

Relieved that it truly wasn't him who'd ruined Reaghan's good mood he told her, "Kesila could try the patience of a saint."

"Could she now?"

"She is rarely told no and she doesn't know how to behave when she is."

The doors opened at Reaghan's floor and she stomped out of the lift without looking back. At her door she swiped her card and pushed it open without waiting for him to assist.

On instinct, he followed her inside.

She tossed the wrap she had been wearing onto the sofa and confronted him. "Sounds like you know her pretty well."

He frowned, sensing he was somehow on shaky ground with Reaghan. "Because of my connection to Edrigu, we were often at the same events so I have known her most of my life."

She crossed her arms. "So you do know her pretty well."

His instincts screamed for retreat. "Define well."

She threw her hands up in the air. "Oh, never mind." She turned to head to the bar. "I don't want to know. I have no right to be asking about old girlfriends."

Realization dawned. She was jealous. Triumph surged throughout his entire being.

He followed her to the bar.

After splashing some amber colored liquid into a crystal glass she tipped it back and swallowed a healthy drink and then cringed. He took the glass from and held her gaze while he drank the rest.

The urge to finally know whether she was his heartmate or not swamped him. The only way to find out was to taste her blood. If he pushed it now he risked scaring her away.

He could enthrall her so that she didn't remember him sampling her, but that idea sat like lead in his gut. It was unimaginable to begin a relationship based on deceit.

He held her gaze and reached for her. His fingers slid across her cheek and into her hair. The pale threads were as soft as silk. He slowly lowered his head until they were only a breath away.

When their lips met the faint echo of his heartbeat quickened.

He skimmed his hand down the back of her neck to the middle

of her back. There he spread his fingers out in a fan to widen his hold on her. The smoky taste of the whiskey clung to her lips.

She slid her hands slid up his chest then grasped the front of his jacket. Instead of being offended or frightened by his forward behavior she pressed herself against him.

Encouraged, he deepened their kiss. He flicked the tip of her tongue with his, silently demanding her surrender. She parried with him, withholding her submission, yet teasing him with a touch of playfulness.

The tingling in his gums warned him what his nature needed. What he yearned for.

Her blood upon his lips.

He dragged his lips across her cheeks and nuzzled her the shell of her ear. She gasped and slumped against him.

He breathed in the scent of her hair –some kind of sweet flower. But it was the smell of her, that which lay beneath her skin, that intoxicated him. He had to taste. He had to know.

His teeth elongated as he nuzzled the side of her neck.

He had to know. He had to know.

He opened his eyes and saw the scar where she had been attacked.

He couldn't do this. Not without her consent.

He gripped the fabric of her dress and fought against his very nature. Likely a little rougher than intended, he plundered her mouth again.

He couldn't get enough. Her kisses were a drug and he was quickly becoming addicted.

"Ouch." She pulled away and touched the side of her lip. On the tip of her finger was a single drop of blood. She looked up at him and gave him a half grin. "I think your fang got me."

He couldn't hear anything against the pounding in his head. His entire world shrank down to the smear of crimson on her lip.

Unable to help himself, he kissed her once again. This time, taking the opportunity to trace her lips with his tongue.

As the faint metallic flavor of her blood hit his mouth, his senses were thrown into a whirlwind. Images flashed in his mind's eyes at an unnatural rate. People he didn't know. Places he had never seen. They spun too fast for him to process what they meant, but he knew they had something to do with Reaghan.

He struggled to regain control.

"Amarande?" Reaghan touched his cheek. "Are you okay?"

He blinked and tried to shake off the barrage of images. His breath caught in his chest. He couldn't draw air. In a panic, he staggered away.

"Amarande?"

He could barely hear Reaghan's voice over the ringing in his ears. When his vision returned at last, he found Reaghan crouched next to him with a worried expression on her face.

"Are you okay?"

"You are the one," he whispered with a touch of awe.

# 15

REAGHAN shook him. "Amarande?"

He groaned.

"Come on big guy." She pressed her head against his chest. She didn't hear anything. Crap, crap, crap. "If you die on me, we'll have more trouble on our hands than either of us want to deal with." She grabbed his shoulders and shook him again.

This time his eyes opened but his gaze seemed distant.

"Can you hear me? Are you all right?" She wondered if her blood, when he pricked her lip, had done something to him. The only vampire-fae pairings she knew of were from legends. But she never recalled hearing that fae blood was poisonous to vampires.

"You." He whispered. "You are the one."

"Yes, it's Reaghan. I think you had a seizure or something. Should I call a doctor?"

He shook his head. "No. No doctor." He sat up, but wobbled a bit.

"Are you sure? You don't look well."

"No. I'm fine." He climbed to his feet.

This time when he looked at her his gaze was clear. And it held a touch of awe.

"What?" she asked.

He touched her face then grimaced. "Nothing."

"That doesn't look like nothing."

"It's fine." He went to the bar and poured himself a drink. He looked at the glass for a moment then drank the content down in one gulp. "I should go."

"I'm not sure you should leave after that..." She gestured to where he had collapsed on the floor. "Whatever that was. Shouldn't you lie down or something?"

"No. I assure you I am perfectly well." He approached her.

"Look." She took his hand and led him to the sofa. "I have an older brother. I know how stupidly stubborn men can be. Especially when there is any possibility of them showing weakness." She forced him to sit then plopped down next to him. "I'm just suggesting you take a few minutes and rest before you go gallivanting off across the castle. If you don't want to stay after you've rested, I won't make you."

His lips twitched. "You do realize that if I really wanted to leave you wouldn't be able to stop me?"

She touched his brow then slid her fingers into his hair. "I know."

He closed his eyes, as if savoring her touch. It bolstered her courage. "But I'd like to think that I could change your mind."

"Perhaps." His eyes slowly opened.

The brown rings around his pupils now had flecks of orange and yellow. Much like a flickering flame. It was really quite lovely.

"I shouldn't stay."

"Why not?" She continued to run her fingers through his hair. She couldn't help herself. The need to touch and comfort him could not be denied.

"Because I now crave you and I don't want those cravings to scare you away."

Her heart fluttered in her chest. "How do you know they will scare me?"

He moved over her, caging her against the seat. "Because I want you in every way a vampire can take his woman." He drew a shuddering breath. "But you already told me you were once attacked by a vampire." He pushed the fabric from her shoulder, exposing her scar. His expression darkened. "I sense your unease, even now." He met her gaze. "I never want you to fear me, Reaghan. Not even for a moment."

She swallowed the lump in her throat. "I wish I could say that I have absolutely no fear of you."

Disappointment flicked through his eyes.

She touched his cheek. "You have had ample opportunity to harm me. I believe that had you wanted to, you would have by now. But…" She bit her lip with indecision. She wanted him. Oh, how she wanted him. Her instincts screamed that she could trust him. And what harm would there be in taking him as a lover? It would only be for the night. Perhaps two. Then they would likely never see each other again.

A part of her cried out at the thought of never seeing him again. Why shouldn't she take this one chance and have a few lovely memories for later?

"But?" He prompted her to continue.

"If I asked you to stay with me tonight, would you have to bite me?" Oddly enough, she wondered if the bite might be pleasant with Amarande. She had often heard it could be downright erotic. But the lingering fear wouldn't let her take that leap.

"No. I would not have to bite you. I mastered my blood cravings centuries ago." His expression turned serious. "Tell me what you want tonight."

It wasn't an easy question when you wanted everything and yet nothing. "To forget about work and family obligations." She glanced at his lips, eager to taste them again. "To get lost in your touch and feel genuine desire."

"That's all?" he asked with a grin.

"That's all it can be."

His smile faded. "I disagree with that limited view, but for now, I can promise to deliver what you think you need."

At her nod, he captured her lips once again and proceeded to make good on his promise.

She wrapped her arms around his chest and clung to him. It had been too long since she had been with a man. It wasn't worth thinking about how long exactly. But Amarande quickly made up for that.

He even kept his fangs from extending again. When he kissed her, her thoughts scattered. She could only feel.

She slipped her hands under the flaps of his jacket to better feel his chest but there was too much fabric in the way. She pushed at the edge of the jacket without ending her kiss. When she couldn't move the fabric far enough out of her way, she became more insistent. Finally he took her hint and sat back onto his knees, taking his weight off of her. He very nearly ripped the jacket off and tossed it aside. Her breath rushed out when he dropped his weight back onto her.

He buried his face in her hair, not far from her neck.

For a fraction of a second she froze. Had he forgotten his promise? When he pressed his face deeper into her hair instead of against her neck a different kind of tension rolled through her. The stubble on his chin scratched her cheek as he dragged his cheek and lips across hers. He nibbled at her lower lip, then slowly inched downward until he was level with her chest.

He skimmed one hand down her chest. "How do you get this thing off?"

"Zipper. In the back."

He fumbled blindly for the zipper. "You have about ten seconds to show me where or I'm ripping it off."

She blinked back the image of him ripping fabric from her body. As hot as that idea sounded, she did like her dress and planned to wear it again. She turned giving him access to her back. Wanting his hands on her again, she pulled her hair to the side so he could find the zipper.

He slid the small tab down her back then peeled the two halves away and paused. "You went all night without a bra?"

She looked over her shoulder at him. "It's one of the advantages of being small chested."

"You're damn lucky I didn't know that until now. The evening would have ended far earlier than you planned." His hands splayed across her shoulder blades then slowly trailed up and out, pushing the straps of her dress off her shoulders as he went. The fabric puddled around her waist as he extended his exploration to the front of her chest.

The buttons of his shirt made a cool contrast against her heated flesh as his chest pressed against her back. He nuzzled her ear as he cupped her breast.

She sagged against his chest, reveling in the way he surrounded her.

He took his time touching and massaging as if he wanted to learn every nuance. Her breath caught when he gave one nipple a firm but gentle pinch.

She let her head fell back against his shoulder when his hand moved to the other breast. With the same tenderness and speed, he explored that one. His free hand came to rest on her thigh, then slowly inched upward to the V between her legs.

He whispered against her ear, "I can't decide if I'm disappointed that you wore panties or relieved."

She chuckled between her gasps as his skillful fingers danced across her nether lips.

Every touch inflamed her. Every stroke made her want him more.

She wanted him inside of her.

She wanted to be possessed by him.

She wanted to taste him.

She wanted to make him as crazed as he made her.

He teased her through her panties, making them wetter by the second. She squirmed and pressed against his hand, needing more. "Amarande," she moaned his name.

"What do you want?"

"More."

"Then more you shall have."

He turned her around so that she faced him once again. Then he leaned her back on the couch and took one of her breasts into his mouth. His tongue traced circles around the tip then sucked the end into his mouth. She gripped the back of his head, praying he didn't stop. By the time he finished loving both breasts she was very near to panting.

Every so slowly, he inched his was downward, pushing her dress out of the way as he went. When he reached her belly button, he reversed directions and moved back up to her breasts. He shifted his position giving him better access to her core.

He slipped one finger inside of her and then used his thumb to put pressure on her clit. She gasped at the sensation and clutched at his shoulders.

He inched downwards until he moved to kneel on the floor beside the sofa. He placed his lips over her clit making her breath catch. He pushed one hand under her and held her by the hip as he licked down to her opening and back up again. She grasped the edge of the sofa so that she had something to keep her anchored as she was flooded with sensations. His lips were magic. Something that powerful should be illegal to deploy on unsuspecting women.

If she had access to her magic she might well have used it. Assuming of course that she probably cast a proper spell at that moment. She doubted she could at that moment though.

His finger pushed in and out of her channel while he licked and sucked at her clit.

Finally the dam she had been clinging to burst and she cried out her pleasure. Stars burst inside her mind's eye and she became adrift in a sensual haze.

Some of the fog lifted when she realized that he was carrying her into the bedroom.

"I hope you are only relocating us."

"That is a certainty. I'm nowhere close to being finished with you."

She rubbed her cheek against his shoulder. "Who's to say that it's not me who isn't finished with you?"

"I should hope not."

 16

HE shifted the way he cradled her then reached for the edge of the bed covers. With a quick flip he tossed them to the end of the bed, out of the way. He lay her gently on the bed and stepped back to take in the picture she made.

She was breath taking. Her disheveled clothes, taut nipples, and flushed skin made an erotic sight. If he lived another three hundred years, he would never see anything so beautiful.

She reached out her hand. "Are you just going to stand there or are you going to join me?"

He fished a condom from his wallet and dropped it on the nightstand. Then he unbuckled his belt and let his pants drop to his knees. "Nothing could keep me from it." He quickly stripped out of the rest of his clothes and sank onto the mattress with her.

"Lift your hips, beautiful."

She dutifully obeyed, allowing him to slide the bunched fabric of her dress down her hips and legs. He tossed it aside then crawled on his hands and knees until he hovered directly over her.

He held her gaze as he slowly lowered his lips to her belly. The tracked a circle around her belly then licked a line all the way up to her neck. There he allowed himself a moment to drink in the scent of her hair. After a quick nip to her ear lobe he moved to her lips.

He reveled in the way she gave herself up to him when they kissed. Part surrender and part challenge.

He skimmed his hand across her breast, then moved lower to the V between her thighs. She was still slick from her earlier release, allowing his finger to slide into her channel with ease. She pressed against his hand and made greedy sounds of need against his lips. He added another finger and pumped in and out while pressing his thumb against her clit.

"Amarande," she whispered.

He loved hearing her call his name. "Tell me what you need, beautiful." He shifted lower so he could run his tongue around one of her nipples.

"I—" She clutched blindly at his shoulders pulling him closer, even as her back arched upward.

He angled his body to keep her pinned in place. "Tell me."

She gasped for air. "You."

Triumph surged in his veins. He snagged the condom and rolled it in place in record time. Then he moved between her legs and angled his cock at her entrance. He pulled one of her knees up then urged her to wrap her leg around his back. With one hand on the mattress near Reaghan's shoulder and the other at her hip, he slowly sank inside of her. He gritted his teeth and fought the urge to rush toward their pleasure.

His instincts drove him to complete the mating. He craved the connection it would bring as well as the physical release. But he refused to it without first explaining to her what was happening. She needed to choose him and he wanted her to choose him of her own free will.

With one slight adjustment, he shifted her other leg, wrapping both around his waist. He rolled his spine, pumping in and out of her body in a steady rhythm. He increased his speed with each thrust until she cried out her pleasure. The walls of her channel gripped his cock and pushed him over the edge. With a hoarse shout, he shuddered his release.

When his faculties returned, he realized he still lay mostly on top of her. For that all too brief moment he surrounded her, held her, possessed her, and yet it was really she who possessed him. Afraid that his weight might be too much for her, he rolled off of her and pulled her firmly against his side.

He dozed for a bit, but the notion of sleeping next to someone was foreign. With all of his previous lovers, one of them left promptly after sex. He never wanted to stay longer than was polite. But tonight, he was loathe to leave. He found he rather liked the way Reaghan curled up next to him with her arm draped across his chest.

He used the quiet time to think about how he wanted to proceed.

He wanted Reaghan. Of that he had no doubt. The unknown there was how receptive she would be to the idea of forever. With him. With a vampire.

The thought that she might turn him down sent cold dread through his entire being. He just needed to make sure that she saw all of the possibilities. If he had to, he would show her the world. Hell, if he wasn't careful, he might just hand it to her on a silver platter.

He grimaced.

First things first. As soon as the lords assembled, he would drop out of the trials. Finding a heartmate was no small thing. The council would understand.

Then he would talk with Reaghan. Tell her everything he knew of heartmates. And then he would convince her to at least give them a chance.

Yes. That would be his plan.

With that decided, he rolled over and nuzzled the side of Reaghan's face.

Her eyes fluttered open and she gave him a shy smile. His heart did strange things. Without words he proceeded to show her everything that he felt. The joy, the excitement, and the hope. Afterward, he fed her wine and fruit that he retrieved from her mini bar as they talked about places they had both been.

Then once more, not long before he sensed the dawn would crest on the horizon, he made love to her. Slowly, tenderly. As if he might never get another chance.

Then after she fell into an exhausted slumber he gently rolled out of the bed and dressed without waking Reaghan. He allowed himself a moment to watch her sleep then slipped out of her room. He scribbled a note letting her know that he needed to return to his own room for the morning hours but that he would find her when he woke.

He hated leaving Reaghan, but it was impossible for him to stay. She might be his heartmate, but he had not secured her connection to him. His years as an Enforcer had driven home the lesson that vampires, not unlike humans, were most vulnerable when they slept. And sleeping somewhere unprotected from not only sun exposure, but also enemies was beyond foolish. He had made far too many enemies in his lifetime to take that risk.

Besides, being separated from Reaghan would likely only be for one more night. If he had his way, he would be removed from the trials before lunch and mated by dinner.

He grimaced. Assuming of course that Reaghan felt the same stirrings. He wouldn't know until he asked her.

Meanwhile, he needed to prepare for the meetings he needed to attend later that day. Part of that preparation included rest and focus. He would do neither if he had stayed. All of his attention would be on her.

The castle was just starting to wake as Amarande made his way to his suite.

He accessed his room then checked that his security measures were still in place and that no one had tampered with them. Granted there were a couple of people who had the skills to bypass his security, but not without a lot of trouble and perhaps a bit of pain. When he was assured that his room was still safe, he reset the alarms, stripped out of his clothes, and climbed into bed.

When he drifted off to sleep he dreamed of a pale haired vixen with lavender eyes.

The next afternoon, he woke with a sense of purpose. He sent a message to Edrigu asking if he could meet with him before the day's meetings. Then he showered and dressed and headed to the hotel lobby, confident that Edrigu would make time for him.

As expected the lobby was yet uncrowded. Most vampires didn't venture out until well after mid-day. As he waited for Edrigu, he grabbed a cup of coffee and a croissant from the café. Then ordered the same for Reaghan and arranged to have it delivered to her room.

He couldn't help, but indulge in the vision

As he exited the café Edrigu caught up to him. "There you are, my boy."

"Good day." Amarande juggled his cup and food in order to clasp hands with his sire.

"Are you just now breaking your fast?"

Amarande shrugged. "I'm afraid so."

"A little late for you isn't it?" Edrigu studied Amarande for a moment. "I see." He smiled knowingly. "So you had a good evening then?"

"Indeed." For some reason Amarande felt a bit like a youngling caught dallying with the neighbor's daughter.

"Is that what you wished to speak to me about?"

"Yes."

Edrigu gestured to the wing where most of the conference rooms were located. "Then perhaps we should move someplace we will have privacy."

"I would appreciate that." Amarande ate his pastry as they walked.

As expected, they had no trouble finding an empty meeting room.

"So tell me what's on your mind," Edrigu said as he took a seat at the table.

Amarande sat his cup on the table next to him as he slid into the chair next to Edrigu. "I have found my heartmate."

Edrigu smiled. "Shaia thought you may have." He tipped his head slightly. "She also said that she might be human. Is that true?"

"Yes."

"The violin player," Edrigu guessed with confidence.

Amarande grinned. "Yes."

"What will you do?"

"I plan to talk with her tonight. To explain everything and pray that she accepts me."

Edrigu nodded in agreement. "I believe that is all that you can do." He leaned closer. "What do you need from me?"

"I merely wanted to get your thoughts on two points. First, I plan to drop out of the trials today. But I had the thought that I might be breaking some protocol with the council. And if so, I wondered if things would go smoother if I remained in the trials without participating in the last few events. As you know, I have hopes of one day leading my own clan. I would need the full support of the council for that. I don't wish to burn any bridges that I don't have to."

"Valid concern. But one I don't think you need to worry about." Edrigu sat back in his chair. "The purpose of the trials is to assist with finding a suitable mate. A heartmate is rare and prized. No one on the council would begrudge you for pursuing yours."

"And if she rejects me?"

"You have done well in the trials and have a solid reputation as one of our best Enforcers. I believe you could still make an advantageous match, if you so choose." Edrigu tapped his finger on the arm of his chair. "Do you believe she will reject you?"

Amarande winced. "I do not really know. Were she vampire, I believe we would not even need to have this conversation. But since she is human – one who was previously attacked by a vampire – I cannot be certain."

Edrigu stiffened. "She was attacked? By whom?"

"I do not have the full story yet. And when she mentioned it, she refused to give me his name. She did say that the council ensured he was punished."

Edrigu frowned. "We get far more reports of humans being attacked than I care to think about so it is possible. You think that is what will make her less receptive of your attachment?"

"That and just knowing that humans do not form the same bonds that we do. I have no idea if she feels anything close to what I feel for her. After all, we only just met."

"Yet she let you feed from her?"

Amarande shook his head. "No."

"Then how can you be certain she is your heartmate?"

"Her lip was cut while we kissed. It only took that one tiny drop of blood for me to know."

"Ah." Edrigu nodded in understanding.

"You never told me however, what a powerful reaction it would be."

"What do you mean?"

"That one tiny drop of blood very nearly knocked me out. I collapsed onto the floor as the images flooded my head. I was completely unprepared for that."

Edrigu frowned. "You saw images? Of what?"

"It was a barrage of people and places. I strongly suspect they were her memories."

Edrigu's frown deepened.

"Surely you saw Shaia's too."

Edrigu shook his head slowly.

Amarande blinked in confusion. "Then what did I see?"

"I don't know exactly. Only she can tell you. If they were not memories, then we need to investigate further." Edrigu tapped his finger on the arm of the chair again. "I will ask some of the other lords if they have ever heard of such a thing happening." Before Amarande could interject, he added, "Discreetly, of course."

"Should I be worried?"

Edrigu regarded him. "Possibly not. But I do recommend proceeding with caution where this girl is concerned. Perhaps you should learn everything you can about her before leaping into the mating ritual with her."

Amarande considered what he knew of her already. He readily

admitted that his knowledge was lacking. If he were investigating someone, he would never move without more information. It would be foolish to do so about something as important as a heartmate. No matter what his instincts said.

"There is one other thing that I was loathe to bring up but perhaps it is relevant after all," Edrigu said.

"What's that?"

"Shaia said that she sensed something was not quite right about your violin player."

Amarande's brows rose in surprise.

"Nothing bad, mind you," Edrigu quickly added. "She said it was her playing. That it was too perfect. Perhaps a touch…otherworldly."

Amarande frowned. If anyone other than Shaia had said that, he would dismiss their comments as jealousy or pettiness. But that was not the case with Shaia. What had she picked up on? He had been so absorbed with Reaghan and his fascination with her, as well as his own performance, he detected nothing.

"It could be nothing. I did not notice anything. But you know how sensitive she is to the things that you and I cannot see."

Amarande nodded then took a sip from his coffee to give himself a moment to collect his thoughts. He didn't want to consider the possibility that Reaghan might be anything except his heartmate, but it would be foolish to move forward blind.

"It is possible that somewhere in her lineage, there was a shifter or one of the many Others." Edrigu shrugged. "There could have possibly been a vampire too."

"Perhaps." Edrigu's explanation made sense. He hoped that would turn out to be the case. "I will take your advice and ask her more about her family as well as those images I saw in my head."

"I believe that would be a smart move." Edrigu got to his feet.

Amarande also stood. "As always, I appreciate your wisdom," he told his sire fondly.

Edrigu clasped Amarande's shoulder. "And I appreciate that you are not so full of yourself that you are unwilling to listen." He shook his head sadly. "Like so many of our young people these days."

They walked to the door.

"Shaia and I will, of course, keep this to ourselves. But I expect you to inform us when you and your mate have everything settled."

"I will." Edrigu and Shaia had always been good to him. Most of the time he wondered what he had done to deserve them. "Now I believe I need to find one of the event coordinators and withdraw from the trials."

Edrigu nodded. "I wish you luck. With everything."

"Thank you."

With a head full of questions, Amarande rushed to find one of the coordinators so he could at least put one part of his plan into motion.

 17

THE delivery of coffee and pastries had been a lovely surprise since she had opted for sleeping in that morning. The tea she prepared in her room when she woke paled in comparison to the sweet, frothy concoction Amarande sent up for her. She smiled as she replayed their night together while she soaked in the oversized tub. Her body ached in more than one place because it had been so long since she had taken a lover. But the aches were not wholly unwelcome.

She took her time with her bath then dressed so that she could get out and look for Eirin while she had free time. Perhaps if she located her early in the evening, she would be able to spend the rest of the night with Amarande. As she looked over the event agenda that she was given when she checked into the hotel for possibilities to search for Eirin, someone knocked on her door.

Her heart skipped a beat hoping it might be Amarande. Disappointment set in when she found one of the hotel staff instead.

"Miss McCarthy?" the young lady in the uniform asked.

"Yes?"

"These were delivered for you." The hotel clerk juggled the vase filled to the brim with pink roses and white lilies. "Shall I bring them in for you?"

Reaghan gasped. "Oh my." She blinked away her surprise. "I, uh... yes, please." She held the door open so the clerk could pass through. In the sitting area, the young lady set the flowers on the table in the center of the room.

"Is this where you would like them?"

"Yes. That will do." Reaghan hurried to the counter where she had left her purse. She grabbed a few bills and handed them to the clerk. "Thank you so much."

After the clerk let herself out, Reaghan searched for a card amid the bright blooms. It read, "Thinking of you. Hope to see you this evening. ~A"

She got a warm feeling all over knowing Amarande had thought of her and made an effort to let her know. No wonder human women loved getting flowers. She practically floated through the rest of the afternoon. Even though she only managed to spot Eirin in passing, she wasn't nearly as frustrated as she might have been.

After fulfilling her obligation to play for a small group of what seemed to be Lady Edrom's friends, she chatted with a few of the ladies and learned what she could about Eirin's significant other. Or, if the ladies were correct, Eirin's intended. The couple was reportedly going through the formalities his family required in order for them to mate. Reaghan was fascinated to learn that their pairing had created quite the scandal within his clan. Apparently, the daughter of one of the clan's senior ranking members thought she should have been chosen instead of Eirin. She created an uproar just before the family left for Tullamore. So much that the clan's sire forbade her from attending the bachelor trials. When that punishment didn't quell the girl's temper-tantrum she was ordered to go live with an aunt in a remote area of the Netherlands until after the birth of Eirin's first child.

The ladies were quick to add that the girl's protest to the marriage was due not only to her desire to marry the next clan lord, but also the fact that he was mating a fae.

Reaghan's curiosity wouldn't let her hold her question in. "What did his family say when they learned the girl was a fae?"

"Nothing of course," one lady told the group.

"Lord Greenwood has always made it clear that he has no quarrels with the fae. Supposedly he attended university with one. And he has remained in touch with him, working deals with from time to time to obtain resources his clan needs to survive."

There were murmurings of understanding amongst the group.

She was so surprised by their reactions that Reaghan had to make an effort to hold her mask of indifference in place.

"Whatever he has been doing seems to be working. As I heard it, his father ran their clan so far into debt that they were living off of nothing but what they could grow in their own back yards. Now the entire clan is healthy and prosperous."

"That's wonderful," Reaghan said. Perhaps she could find out who Lord Greenwood had befriended when she returned home. They would likely have good insight into working with and interacting with vampires.

"I do hope those two young people make it," one of the matrons added. "I am inclined to agree with Lord Greenwood. The only way we will survive is if we broaden our horizons and allow new connections to blossom and grow. Our blood pool has grown stale. It needs revival. And our young people are the ones who can do it."

One of the other ladies nodded enthusiastically. "I believe you are right, Majorie. I just hope I live to see our family tree revived before I pass on."

"I often wonder if the reason that no one finds their heartmate any more is because they are so rarely sought beyond our own kind."

"I have wondered that myself." The other ladies nodded sadly.

"Heartmate?" Reaghan asked.

The matron sitting next to Reaghan patted her hand. "Our apologies, dear. A heartmate is a bit like what you humans often call a soulmate. Someone fate specifically intended for us."

Vampires believed in destined mates? Why had she never heard of this before?

The woman across the table added, "But the connection is intense. To the point that the mates know what each other feels and sometimes even thinks without asking."

Another lady said, "The connection is so deep that when one mate dies or is killed, the other follows shortly after."

"Did any of you find your heartmate?" Reaghan asked.

They all shook their heads. One of them gestured to Lady Edrom with her tea cup. "Marceline did."

"So did Shaia Moreschi," the lady across from her said.

"There are a hand full of others. But it is rare," the lady to Reaghan's right pointed out.

"Seems to be even more rare now." All of the ladies nodded their agreement.

How sad. If what they said was true, were vampires, like the fae, slowly dying out? That might explain the imbalanced male-to-female ratio in the trials.

Instead of answering questions, the information Reaghan gathered only led to new ones. She wasn't sure if she was more surprised by the fact that not only were the fae not hated, but actually welcomed by at least some. That news was so far from what she had been told that she didn't know where to turn for answers. Good answers. Impartial answers.

Her head spun for the remainder of the luncheon. Afterwards she packed up her instrument, accepted the ladies' thanks, then followed the group back into the bustling hallway. Just as she merged into the flow of people moving through the hallway someone grabbed her arm. She gasped and pulled her case up in front of her as a shield.

"Whoa. Sorry," Amarande immediately let go of her. "I didn't mean to scare you. I guess you didn't hear me when I called."

"No." She smiled with relief when she saw who it was. Amarande tugged at her violin case until she let him take it. Then she put her hand over her heart where it pounded against her chest. "I guess I was lost in my thoughts."

He lifted the case. "I take it you just played for someone?"

"Yes. Lady Edrom and a group of her friends." She fell into step beside him. "We had tea as well."

He nodded in understanding. "So what, if I may ask, has you so distracted?"

She waved her hand in the air dismissively. "Just some of the gossip the ladies were sharing."

"Anything about me?"

"Surprisingly, no." She tilted her head. "But your sire and his wife, I believe, were mentioned."

"If they had anything to say that would make me angry, don't share it."

She shook her head. "It was nothing negative at all. The ladies were discussing what they called heartmates."

Amarande stiffened.

"Apparently they are one of only a few couples who have found their heartmates."

"Yes. That is true." He looked straight ahead. "And did they tell you what heartmates were?"

"Only a little. I had never heard of the term before so I asked."

"And what did you think?"

"I found the idea fascinating. But also a little sad."

He finally looked at her. "Why sad?"

"Because it sounds as if it is a very special bonding or connection but it doesn't happen very often."

"No. It doesn't."

He stopped walking when they reached the lobby. "I—" He paused and glanced at the people milling about them. A tiny V formed in the middle of his brow.

"You...?" she prompted him to continue.

"Would you like to go for a walk with me later?"

She glanced at the windows. "It's rather late for walk, isn't it?"

His lips twitched in a partial smile. "Not for a vampire, no."

Distracted by the possibility of kissing those lips, she mumbled, "I guess that is true."

"There is something that I'd like to discuss with you in private."

What could he possibly want to talk about that required privacy? She gestured to the lift. "We can go to my room if you'd like. Or yours."

That turquoise sparkle she had come to recognize as a sign he was aroused returned to his eyes. "I fear there are far too many temptations in either of our rooms for me to keep my thoughts straight." He glanced away, in almost a shy manner. "Besides, there is a place at the base of the cliffs, on the beach, that I like to go whenever I visit Tullamore. It is spectacular in the moonlight. I'd like to share it with you, if you have any interest."

She had far more interest than was good for her but he didn't need to know that. "Very well."

"I need to take care of something for Edrigu before we go, but I can swing by your room in about an hour. Unless you have other obligations before then?"

"No, I don't. I will need to eat later but that can wait until after our walk." She smiled up at him. "Perhaps you can join me?"

He dipped his head. "That sounds just about perfect."

"I'll see you in an hour then." He returned her case to her then hurried away.

Disappointed that he didn't kiss her as she hoped, she turned and headed to the lift. Along the way she had the feeling that she was being watched. As discreetly as possible she looked for the source, but could not spot anyone paying her any attention.

The feeling vanished as soon as the doors to the lift closed. Perhaps she was just being over sensitive. The hotel lobby was not the best place for Amarande to flaunt his affair with a human. Especially when his purpose for being at the meeting was to find a wife. Or mate. Or whatever they called each other. It was possible someone had been watching to see if he would accompany her to her room.

As much as she didn't want to think about him with another woman, it would be unfair to hope that he didn't find one as a result of the trials. After all, she would be returning to her own world tomorrow. It was very possible she might never see him again.

Unless she did something to change that.

But what could she do?

She spent the next hour rolling ideas around in her head about how she could make her way back to the mortal plane. Assuming of course that Amarande wanted to continue their relationship.

Her instincts said that was what he wanted to discuss with her.

Never mind that he thought she was human. Once her assignment for the queen was complete she would likely be able to tell him the truth. But would he believe her? Would he want anything to do with her if he knew she was fae? The ladies at the luncheon indicated the fae were not considered to be monsters so perhaps she stood a chance.

At almost one hour on the dot, Amarande came for her. Once again, she was disappointed that he didn't kiss her. That didn't bode well for their topic of conversation.

"You may want to bring a sweater with you. It can get pretty windy on the cliff," he advised her.

She couldn't very well tell him that she didn't get cold like humans did. "That is probably a good idea." Even though her excitement to venture out with him had been dampened, she hurried to the bedroom and grabbed the first thing she could find. "Okay. I am ready."

He gestured for her to proceed him, holding the door open for her as they left her room.

He was somewhat quiet as they ventured out of the hotel. Enough to make her doubt her earlier thoughts about seeing him again after her assignment.

"How was your day?" she asked to fill in some of the quiet.

"Fine."

She waited, hoping he would elaborate, but he didn't. "How did your events go today? Are you still at the top of the trials?"

"I don't know. I didn't participate in any of the events today."

She frowned. "I thought you had various challenges all weekend."

"Some do."

Her heart sank. "Are you doing so well then that you're able to skip some of the events?"

"Something like that."

It finally occurred to her that he might have asked her to walk with him in order to break things off because he had found his mate. She swallowed her disappointment.

He was handsome. The way he dressed and his carriage hinted he was at least well off, if not wealthy. The fighting skills he demonstrated in the arena proved he would be a good protector. What more could a woman ask for in a husband?

Love, her heart whispered even as it ached at the thought of him being with anyone else.

They made it to a fork in the path. One trail led deeper into the trees but the other ran along the edge. Tiny solar lights scattered along the stone walkway cast a faint glow making it easy to remain on the path. Even without the lights, Reagan's fae senses allowed her to see fairly well in the dark.

She squinted at the sign that had been posted at the fork.

"This is the path that will take you to the shore," Amarande told her without even glancing at the weather beaten wood post.

"You seem to know this pathway well. I guess you've walked this way a few times?"

"I have."

"Do you often bring your paramours with you?"

"Actually, I've never brought anyone." He glanced her way then focused on the trail again. "I like being outside. And there is something about the water on the shore that relaxes me."

Her heart fluttered in response. She liked the idea of being the first to be asked to go with him to a place that soothed him.

They hadn't gone far when a twig snapped with an echoing crunch somewhere in the trees to their right. Amarande stiffened and he turned his head ever so slightly but didn't stop.

Reaghan's instincts went on alert. There was a variety of animals in the woods -most of them harmless- and none of them could best her. However, her gut cautioned her that she and Amarande were being watched. Perhaps even stalked. But by what? Or... by whom?

"So tell me about yourself," he prompted her.

"What would you like to know?" She kept one eye on the surrounding foliage.

"Where are you from? Who are your parents? What did you want to be when you grew up?"

"Do you want my height, weight, and blood type too?" she chuckled nervously, wondering why he would be asking such things.

"No. I've already marked your height and I can get that other information off your driver's license later. I want to know about you and what makes you tick."

"Oh. Well…" She cleared her throat to buy herself some time. She needed to put a human spin on her background without outright lying to him. "My mother comes from an affluent family. She's never worked. But she is active with many of the local…" She made a circling motion with her hand as if it would help her find the word she wanted. "Oh, I suppose you could call them social and political groups."

"Do you have any siblings?"

"Yes. One older brother and one younger sister. My sister is still attending lessons."

"Lessons? You mean she's still in school?"

"Yes. Schooling. She's the baby of the family." As they neared a darkened area of the trail, the hair on the back of her neck stood on end. "What about y—?" A roar cut off her question. It was followed by snapping and crashing tree limbs.

Amarande pushed her behind him. "Run back to the castle," he ordered.

"I'm not leaving you out here alone!"

He glanced back at her. His eyes burned with an eerie crimson glow and his face had contorted into a fierce expression. "Go!"

She sensed the push of his compulsion, but it was no match against her own magic.

Amarande's distraction gave the attacker a chance to tackle him to the ground. In a haze of fur and fangs, Amarande not only defended himself but went on the offensive. Bone cracked and fabric tore as he wrestled and punched his attacker.

"Well look what we have here."

Reaghan tore her gaze away from Amarande to face the new threat. Three more shifters stepped out of the thick foliage.

"What do you want with us?" she demanded.

"There was nothing in our orders about you. Only your boyfriend there." The hairy creature's words slurred ever so slightly. Likely because of its elongated snout.

"The way I see it, she's a freebie," one of the others said with a leer.

The third hairy advanced on her. "Maybe she's a runner." His grotesque snorting laugh made her skin crawl. "You know I like it when they run."

"Yeah. Go ahead blondie." The second one moved to her right just a bit. "We dare you to run."

She glanced at Amarande.

"Don't worry, baby," the first male taunted her. "We don't plan to kill him. Not yet anyway."

"Not if he does what he's supposed to."

"But if he doesn't..." The third one laughed again.

She took a step backwards and keeping her eye on all three of them as well as Amarande's fight. But the three advancing on her fanned out too far for her to watch at the same time.

When one of them reached for her, she surprised him by not only knocking his hand away, but following up with a solid kick to the side of his knee. The sound of crunching bone was oddly satisfying.

The shifter howled in pain. "She kicked me!"

"Don't be a pussy, Drax. Just grab her," the first one said.

"I'm going to do more than grab her this time." He rushed for her, but she hopped just out of his reach. This time she landed a blow to the back of his head.

"What the fuck, bitch?"

"Drax, you're such an idiot." The first one advanced on her. He snatched at her jacket, but she spun away. "What the—" He tried to grab her again, but she jerked away. His claws tore through her jacket with a rip.

"Reaghan, run!" Amarande shouted at her. It was too late for running and she knew it.

From the corner of her eye she saw Amarande jerk the shifter's arm behind its back then he sank his teeth into its neck.

She switched her focus back to her own attackers in time to see the other two shifters close in. The one closest to her grabbed her and wrapped his arm around her neck. The second grabbed her flailing arm. The third one went for her legs. She stifled her cry even though she hurt in several places. She didn't want to distract Amarande from his fight.

She heard a tearing of flesh and prayed Amarande had finished off the shifter since she could no longer see him. "Let her go!" Amarande bellowed. His voice was much deeper and carried a touch of power.

"Not so fast, Romeo. We've been asked to send you a message loud and clear."

Reaghan struggled against her attackers but they were surprisingly strong. Then again, so was their odor. The combination of wet dog and dirty shoes permeated her senses made her gag. She didn't want to give away her non-human origins, but she feared she would soon be left with no choice.

Fae law forbid revealing their true form to humans except when in mortal danger. She felt this situation might be considered dangerous but perhaps not mortally so. Then again...these were not humans she was dealing with.

"What message are you supposed to deliver to me?" Amarande asked the shifters.

"You must not try to complete the trials. If you do, there will be consequences."

"Is that right?" Amarande took a menacing step in their direction.

One of the shifters pressed a claw against her neck. "Watch it Romeo. I'd hate for your little girlfriend here to get cut and bleed out before you could indulge yourself."

Amarande froze. "Let her go."

"I don't think so." The one with the claw jerked his head toward the body on the ground. "That was my cousin you killed."

"Your cousin should have thought twice about attacking us. Now let her go."

"I don't think you're in a position to be giving us orders."

Light glinted off metal as the third shifter pulled a gun from his jacket and leveled it on Amarande.

"Drax, strip off her trousers." The first one leered. "Let's all get a good look at what kind of treasure we're holding here."

Amarande hissed in warning and his hands balled into fists.

The one named Drax pawed at her waistband, making her gag from the overwhelming odors surrounding her.

"Enough," Reaghan declared then sent a blast of energy from her center. The two shifters close to her flew backwards and crashed into the ground. Even Amarande and the third shifter staggered a few steps back. She conjured a ball of blue flame and threw it at the shifter with the gun. He screamed and clutched at the hand that had been holding the weapon.

She conjured another ball and directed it at the other two shifters.

It scooped them up then floated to the top of a nearby tree where it dropped them. They screamed and clutched at branches trying to find a perch before they plummeted to the ground.

"You're not—" Amarande's mouth hung open in surprise.

"She's not human." A man said from somewhere behind her.

# 18

AMARANDE shook off his surprise and stepped between Reaghan and the new threat. "Who's there?"

"It's Callum." The man emerged from the shadows with both hands raised in a peaceful gesture. "Stand down."

"What do you want?" Amarande asked, less than politely.

"Fighting on Tullamore land always catches my attention. I came to see what was going on."

Reaghan frowned. "What exactly did you see?"

"Nothing that I will be repeating, Mistress Reaghan of Owin."

Reaghan gasped in surprise.

What did Callum call her? He had a really bad feeling he was missing something.

Callum's eyes glowed silver when he faced Amarande again. "Are you all right?"

"Yes." Amarande took Reaghan's hand. "Nothing that a short rest won't fix anyway."

"And perhaps a shower?" Reaghan suggested.

Both men looked at her in question.

She gestured to the place where the shifters had been. "They were rather smelly. I feel like I've been rolled over by a dog that had been outside in the rain."

"That, at least, is an easy fix. Unfortunately dealing with these four will take a little more care so that we don't have an international incident on our hands." Callum leveled his hardened gaze on Amarande. "Do you know why they attacked you?"

"They said it was a warning for me to not complete the trials."

Callum's eyes glowed faintly again. "The bachelor trials? Why would they care if you competed or not?"

Amarande scowled up at the shifters who were still stuck in the tree. "One of the many questions I'd like to have an answer to."

"The even stranger thing is that their warning came after I dropped out of the competition."

"You dropped out?" Reaghan exclaimed.

"Interesting," Callum said at the same time. "You will notify the council that shifters attacked you."

The fact that Callum issued directives rather than asking questions tweaked an already sensitive nerve. "Of course."

"Fighting is not allowed on Tullamore land."

"We were only defending ourselves!" Reaghan protested.

Callum held up his hand. "I don't mean this incident."

Irritation ran hot through Amarande's veins. "He was reminding me that I cannot seek revenge while I am on property."

"Even if they provoke you again." Callum's warning was not at all subtle.

"I will remember," Amarande told him through gritted teeth. He would never admit it, but it was probably a good thing Callum had reminded him of Tullamore's no-fighting rule. If he found who arranged the attack, there was a high probability he would give in to his base instincts.

"Go ahead and return to the castle before anyone else comes. I will take care of this." Callum gestured to the shifters.

"You have my thanks," Amarande said even though it galled him to do so. He took Reaghan's hand and tugged her in the direction they had come. "I'll walk you back to your room." His tone held no room for argument.

"What about you?"

"I need to notify the council what happened. But I can do that while you shower."

"Will you stay with me?"

Images of Reaghan naked and wet flashed through his mind. "I'm not sure that would be wise. But nor do I like the idea of you being alone." He cast her a sideways glance. "Although, you certainly handled yourself well."

"Girl has to do what a girl has to do," she muttered.

His scowl deepened. She was fae. How did he not see that? Normally he could detect a fae glamour but he had not seen a single sparkle or glow on her. Had he been completely taken in by her? And more importantly, why?

"Were you going to tell me that you are fae?"

She sighed. "In truth, no."

Not the answer he wanted to hear. "Why not?"

"My queen forbid me from revealing my true nature to anyone. And, quite frankly, I doubted you'd be around long enough for it to matter."

A muscle twitched in his jaw.

"What are you going to do about those shifters and whoever sent them?" she asked.

"Nothing right now."

"What about later?"

"That depends on the council."

"Does the council tell you what you can and can't do?"

"No more than your queen, it would seem."

She met his angry glare. "Fair enough."

He grunted in response but neither of them said anything else as they passed through the hotel lobby and up to her room. At the door, he stopped her from going farther in. He held up one finger to silence her question. "Let me check first," he whispered.

Unless he was mistaken she rolled her eyes as he walked away. He did a quick search of each room then returned and gave her a brisk nod. "It's fine."

She immediately went to the bar. "Would you like a drink?"

"Yes, but not from the bar." Despite everything he learned tonight, he still wanted her.

She suddenly looked up from pouring the wine which made her splash some onto the counter.

"Careful." He dabbed the drop she had spilled with his finger. "You're wasting perfectly good wine." Then he lifted that finger to her lips.

"What are we doing here?" she whispered.

"I don't know exactly." He gazed deep into her eyes. "You're fae. I should hate you."

"Why?"

"Because..." He grimaced. "Because I was there for the war." He turned away, caught unexpectedly by old memories. "I was young. I didn't fight but I was a victim of it."

"We all were," she said softly.

"The fae killed my parents, my sister, my original Sire, and most of my original clan."

"I—" She bit her lip, stopping whatever she started to say.

"You what?" he asked softly then touched her cheek.

"I just don't know what to do," she whispered.

His head hurt with all of the thoughts bouncing around in there. "I hope you don't think that I do." He tentatively slid his fingers into her hair then let his hand drop. "I came here this weekend with one goal in mind. But meeting you has clouded that picture." He walked toward the fireplace. "It shouldn't, but it has. Tell me the truth. Did you plan to distract me this weekend? To ensure I did not complete the trials?"

"What?" She blinked in surprise. "No. I didn't even know you existed before this weekend."

"Did someone send you?" he asked in a rush.

She bit her lip.

Anger and disappointment swirled inside of him. He marched to the fireplace.

"Someone did send me," she finally admitted. "But it has absolutely nothing to do with you."

He narrowed his gaze on her. "Then what does it have to do with?"

"I cannot tell you."

He marched back to her. "Can't or won't."

"Can't."

Frustration sizzled in his gut. "Why not?"

"Because my queen commanded me."

He studied her expression, looking for any clue that she was lying. Not finding any, he stomped away again. He leaned one hand against the fireplace mantle and silently counted to five to calm himself. "Can you at least tell me if any of the council lords are in danger?"

"Not immediately. But you all may be if I fail in my mission."

His head snapped up. "Tell me," he demanded.

She shook her head. "I cannot."

He gritted his teeth. Then a horrible thought occurred. "Does your mission involve killing anyone?"

"What? No." She cringed. "Unless…"

"Unless?"

"Unless I or…" She looked away. "Or any other fae citizen are in immediate danger."

Some of the tension drained from him. "So you're looking for someone."

Her eyes widened when she realized what she'd revealed. She held up a finger. "I didn't say that."

"Another fae." He advanced on her. She took a step back. "Is this fae you're looking for dangerous to anyone here?"

"No." The wall behind her prevented her from going farther.

He caged her in by placed one hand against the wall on either side of her shoulders. "You seem awfully certain of that."

"I am."

He studied her expression. Her beauty and sincerity held the power to disarm him in a blink. She was dangerous to him and she didn't even know it. "Why you?" he whispered, mostly to himself.

"Because my queen trusted no one else to learn the truth."

He blinked away his stray thoughts. "The truth about what?"

She shook her head, but said nothing.

He let his forehead drop and press against hers. He closed his eyes. "Tell me something. Anything. Prove to me that I was not part of whatever it is that you're doing here. And for God's sake, tell me why I shouldn't drag you in front of the Council of Lords and let them figure out what to do with you."

"I know you have no reason to believe me but you were never a part of my assignment. I swear it. You were..." She touched his cheek. "An unexpected bright spot in a sea of turmoil."

Once again he saw nothing but sincerity in her eyes. But at this point he doubted everything he knew and felt about her.

"I am also willing to swear that as soon as I talk with the person I came to find, I will leave. I have only until sun rise on the third day to do it anyway."

He ignored the part about her leaving and focused on the rest. "You have to talk to some fae who just happens to be here at the vampire gathering."

"Yes."

"But you can't tell me why."

She shook her head.

"Because it is extremely important, yet secret."

"Yes." She cringed. "Even though that does make it sound rather...unimportant."

"Yes, it does." He sighed and took a step back, let his hands drop away from the wall. "Since you aren't breaking any laws by being here, I see no reason why I should stop you from seeking out one of your own people. But, for entirely personal reasons, I must insist that you refrain from going anywhere tonight. I need to report the shifter attack to the council and find out who or what was behind it."

He held up his hand cutting off what was likely going to be a protest. "I know whatever you're doing is important, but until I know the extent of the threat we encountered tonight, it just isn't smart to put yourself in danger any more than you probably already are."

She crossed her arms and scowled at him.

"With all that fae magic, I'm surprised your queen couldn't find this person on her own."

Reaghan shook her head. "Our powers aren't unlimited. And when we cross from our world into the human realm, they don't work quite the same."

"I assumed you guys could do pretty much anything you wanted."

"That is most certainly untrue. Especially when there are, as the humans generalize it, politics involved."

He sighed. "Great." He rubbed one hand across his face hoping to push the blossoming headache away. "Every time politics are involved my job always gets ten times harder."

He took in everything he could about her. He wanted to see what he hadn't before, but in truth, nothing seemed different. "Don't make me regret not turning you over to the council." It was part plea and threat.

She gave him a stiff nod.

With that he hurried out of her suite to make his report to the council. Before he did something really stupid like asking her to say to hell with everything and running away with him.

19

REAGHAN paced the confines of her suite. Even the hot shower she had taken had done little to calm her.

Why she was following anyone's orders other than her king or queen was baffling. Much less someone from the human realm. And a vampire, at that. The shifters who attacked them had very obviously been after him. She had merely been in the way.

She didn't blame him for wanting to find out who was behind it and why. The shifters said it was because of the trials. Even though Amarande said he had withdrawn from them.

Why had he withdrawn?

The only logical reason for him to do so would be if he had found a perspective mate. She cringed. Her earlier suspicions about why he had invited her for the walk to talk seemed even more likely.

Whoever sent the shifters clearly didn't know he had withdrawn. It must have happened quite recently. Perhaps even earlier that day? After all he had spent most of the night with her.

She frowned. So when had he met this perspective mate then?

She stomped across the room to the event calendar. She scanned the contents but nothing there gave her any indication of his activities earlier that day. Something must have happened between the time he left her suite and found her in the hallway earlier.

She threw the brochure down in a huff. What difference did it make? She was merely a distraction to him. Just like he was supposed to be for her.

Her heart whispered, *liar.*

The event list had said something about a ladies' spa day being held the next day. That would be a good opportunity to search for Eirin. And the idea of a little pampering wouldn't hurt either.

She used the hotel phone to make an appointment then went to get ready for bed. Before climbing into bed she reinforced the wards around her suite in case the shifters decided to come looking for her. She felt guilty for not informing Pwyll of the incident with them, but the last thing she wanted or needed was her big brother showing up and taking over her assignment.

As she slipped under the covers, memories of the previous evening with Amarande assaulted her. She tossed and turned for what seemed like hours before finally falling into a fitful slumber.

She dreamed of war and wolves, court intrigue and deception. But all throughout, a pair of turquoise eyes followed her, giving her strength and comfort.

The next morning she rose and conjured a light breakfast for herself. Then she used her magic to make herself presentable for the day. Now that her powers were unbound, there was little point in not using them. Besides, she needed to reinforce her glamour before rejoining any of the vampires.

She would have to be extra careful now that she had broken Caoilfhinn's binding on her powers.

Part of her was sad that Amarande had not come to her last night. But if he was now committed to a mate, it wouldn't be right for him to do so. Still she was curious what he had learned about their attackers.

The phone for the suite rang.

"Yes?" She answered foolishly hoping it might Amarande.

"Miss McCarthy? This is Bella with the Seacrest Spa." Disappointment sat like a lump in Reaghan's belly. "I'm calling to confirm your appointment with us at noon."

"Oh, yes. I will be there."

"Okay. Thank you very much. We'll see you then."

She finished her coffee and headed to the spa. As she crossed the lobby foyer she spotted Amarande speaking with a two other vampires. She kept her focus on her destination, all the while hoping he didn't notice her.

Just as she reached the safety of the spa doors Amarande caught her. "I thought you agreed to stay in your room," he growled in her ear.

"I did. Last night. Today, I have an appointment." She pulled the door open and breezed through.

The girl at the counter smiled when she looked up, but her smile faltered when she spotted Amarande and what was likely his scowl.

"Hi, I'm Reaghan McCarthy. I have an appointment."

The girl clicked a few buttons on her keyboard. "Yes, ma'am. I'll let your attendant know you're here."

"Thank you."

"How long will your appointment take?" Amarande asked Reaghan while the girl spoke to someone on the phone.

"Several hours." She took a deep breath to try and dispel her irritation. "Why?"

"Because I wasn't finished talking to you."

"Hmmm. I would be interesting to hear what you learned about our..." She glanced at the girl behind the counter. "Our guests last night, but I'm afraid it will have to wait. I'm sure you won't want to give your chosen fiancée the wrong impression by being seen in here with me. So, how about if I come find you in a few hours?"

"My what?" He blinked in confusion.

"Miss McCarthy?" Reaghan turned to see who had called her. A handsome young man wearing a white, fitted t-shirt and matching pants stood in the doorway with an expectant look. The material of his shirt and pants clung to his muscular chest and legs as if it had been painted on. "I'm Connor. I'll be your attendant this evening."

She blinked back her own surprise. Based on the amount of muscle mass she'd wager Connor did more than just spa treatments. Perhaps a bit of Caber tossing? "It's lovely to meet you Connor. I'm so looking forward to this."

Behind her, Amarande growled. She shot him a dark look over her shoulder.

Connor smiled and gestured for her to proceed him. "Right this way." After they passed through the doorway he asked. "Are you with the convention we have in house this weekend?"

"Yes, I am."

"We've had several of the ladies take advantage of our offerings today," Connor told her.

"It's hard to turn down an opportunity to be pampered," Reaghan said. "Are many of them still here?"

"I believe we do have quite a few at various stations. We try to spread everyone out so that no one waits long."

If all of the clients were spread out, that would make finding Eirin more challenging. But at least there was a chance.

Connor stopped where two hallways intersected. He gestured to one path. "The changing room is at the end of the hall, on the right. You'll find robes and slippers for your use. Feel free to leave your things in any of the available lockers."

When Reaghan realized Amarande was following them she faced him. "What are you doing?"

"I'm going with you."

She frowned. "You can't come back here."

Connor interrupted them, "Spouses and partners are allowed in the massage room if it makes the client more comfortable."

Amarande's teeth glittered when he smiled. "See? I'm allowed."

She crossed her arms over her chest and shot him a look daring him to argue. "You're neither my spouse nor my partner." She added emphasis to the word, my.

Connor glanced between the two of them. "My apologies. I just assumed..."

Amarande turned his focus on the human. "I am permitted. You will not make a fuss or try to evict me from her room."

Connor's eyes softened as if he were slipping into a dreamy state.

"Stop that," Reaghan hissed at Amarande. "You can't just go around making people do what you want them to do. It's not right."

"I'm not leaving you alone with Conan the Barbarian while you're lying on a table mostly naked." He leaned closer. "It just isn't going to happen. Adjust."

She harrumphed. "I don't know what difference it makes to you. You're the one getting engaged or mated or whatever to someone else." She stomped off for the changing room.

The man is simply infuriating. Why should he care whether she got a massage or not? Hell, if she were to jump Connor's bones, what difference should it make? He was the one getting engaged.

She cringed. Although, technically, she was too. At least as far as everyone at home thought.

How was she supposed to tip-toe around the spa looking for Eirin with him lurking over her shoulder?

Uggg. Men.

 20

THAT woman was going to drive him mad.

He had hoped to have the discussion he was supposed to have with her the night before. But it seemed he was being derailed once again.

Amarande waited for her, not so patiently, in what he assumed was the massage room. There was an oddly shaped table in the center of the room that had been covered with a pristine white sheet. Another sheet and a thin blanket lay folded at one end. The lights had been turned down and soft music flowed from hidden speakers. While he approved of the fact that there were no windows he didn't care for only having access to one exit.

He inspected the oils and lotions that had been stored on the built-in shelves. But it didn't take long to overwhelm his hyperactive vampire senses.

Reaghan entered, wearing a thick white robe and plush slippers. She had pulled her hair up into a bun on top of her head. She shot him a look of annoyance.

"What are you still doing here?" She closed the door behind her and came to stand next to the massage table.

"I needed to speak to you."

"What could possibly be so important that it cannot wait a couple of hours?"

He frowned as his gaze slipped lower, down to her bare feet.

"What?" She asked as she moved to the other side of the table.

"What are you wearing under that robe?"

"Nothing. Why?"

He growled.

"You do realize that's the best way to get a massage, right?" She grabbed the white sheet from the foot of the table, she shook it open then did the same with the blanket. She glanced at him, then the door, then rolled her eyes and let out an exasperated sigh. After turning her back to him, she loosened the belt on the robe and let the garment slide down her arms, then tossed it onto the nearby chair.

His mouth went dry watching her climb onto the table, arrange herself face-down with only a much too thin sheet for cover.

He prowled closer. "I already told you that I am not comfortable with Conan—"

"His name is Connor," she corrected him.

"With Conan, or any man, putting his hands on you."

She raised her head and looked at him. "Why? This isn't a sexual exercise. This is purely for relaxation and therapy." She let her head flop back down and she closed her eyes. "You should try it some time."

"I can think of a dozen better ways to relax."

She harrumphed.

A knock at the door caught their attention.

"Come in," she called out.

Connor entered. His glaze landed briefly on Amarande then returned to Reaghan. He began to gather supplies from the shelf behind the table. "Miss McCarthy, do you have any spots that require particular attention or that you would like for me to work more than the others?"

"I am experiencing an unusual pain in my neck today." She picked her head up from the oval shaped pillow and shot a glare in his direction. "But other than that, nothing in particular."

"And do you prefer a light touch or deeper penetration?"

Amarande wiped his hand over his face. Was Connor asking that in a deliberately crude way? Or did he make it sounded implicit on purpose?

"Perhaps a little of both. I'll let you know if you need to go deep."

"I'm going to start at the top and work my way down. Then we'll turn you over and work the other side."

"That sounds wonderful."

Amarande growled and moved away to stand in the corner where he could keep an eye on everything the oversized massage therapist did.

Connor slathered his hands with some kind of lotion and rubbed them together. Amarande detected lavender and some kind of citrus.

As soon as Connor touched Reaghan, Amarande realized he'd made a mistake following them. Watching Connor run his hands across Reaghan's arms triggered a myriad of foreign feelings. Jealousy. Possession. And even insecurity. Even though he knew Connor worked the muscles in her shoulder and arm in a clinical fashion, it didn't help. Every stroke ratcheted Amarande's tension higher.

No one should be touching his mate except for him.

He clenched his jaw. They may not be formally mated, but he knew without a doubt that she was his. His and his alone. He just needed to convince her of that fact.

The million dollar question was, would she accept him?

And if she did, could their mating be completed? His gut screamed that yes, it could, should, and would be. Sooner rather than later, if he had his way.

He was still reeling from the fact that she thought he was to be mated to someone else. Where had she gotten that idea? As soon as he got her alone he would disprove that notion.

He turned away and tried to block out the reality of someone else touching his mate. If he didn't watch every stroke, perhaps he could deal with it.

Connor's voice droned in the back ground as he asked some of the most mundane questions. How long would she be staying at the hotel? Had she visited the local village? What was her favorite part of Tullamore so far?

Amarande listened with a half an ear until it occurred to him that perhaps this was an opportunity to learn more about his mate. But how did he get the oaf to ask the questions he wanted answers to?

He could impose his will on the man, but to do so, Reaghan would hear the initial commands. And if she did, she might resist answering truthfully.

Connor finished working on her back then carefully pulled the sheet and blanket up covering her. Next he tucked the sheet around one leg while carefully exposing the other. It was somewhat impressive how he used the fabric as a barrier to maintain Reaghan's privacy but when he tucked it firmly between her thighs Amarande very nearly tossed him from the room.

Reaghan sighed softly as Connor worked the muscles in her legs then her feet. When he finished he moved around the table and held the sheet up like a shield so she could turn over onto her back.

Amarande's jaw ached from clenching it so hard.

Once she was situated on her back and the sheet lay over her chest, covering her all the way down to her pretty toes, Connor placed a folded cloth over her eyes.

Amarande pulled two fifty pound notes from his pocket and approached the table. Connor looked up from his preparations in question. Amarande held the notes up so Connor could see what he held, then used them to point to the door.

Connor looked down at Reaghan.

Amarande tipped his head toward the door, with as much of a reassuring look as he could muster.

Connor shrugged, handed Amarande the oil, took the money, and quietly slipped out of the room.

Amarande rolled the sleeves of his shirt up, then coated his hands with the oil and moved her Reaghan's side. He reached for her shoulder but as soon as their skin came in contact, he felt the same warmth and awareness of her being as always.

She gasped and reached for the cloth covering her eyes.

"No." He grabbed her hand and stopped her from taking it. "Just let me. Please."

She shook her head knocking the towel from her face. When she sat up, she clutched the sheet to her chest. "We can't do this."

"Why not?"

"Because you're…" She waved her hand at him. "You're getting married or picking a bride, or whatever."

"What are you talking about?" He moved around to the front of the table to stand in front of her.

"You dropped out of the trials. I assumed that meant you had picked out your bride and came to some agreement. Am I right?"

"Partially."

"Well that's fine because I'm engaged to someone else, anyway."

"You're what?" he growled as red coated his vision. Watching someone else touch his mate had been hard enough. Hearing that she was attached to another man was more than he could take.

Her eyes widened and she drew back. "Well, technically, anyway."

"Technically? You either are or you aren't promised to someone else. Which. Is. It." He caged her in by placing his fists on the bench on either side of her. Then he leaned in until their noses very nearly touched and stared deep into her eyes. He willed her to tell him the truth. At the same time he silently pleaded for it to not be true.

She tried to push him away but he refused to budge. She rolled her eyes and sighed. "My father did promise me to someone. The son of a...colleague."

He felt her answer like a blow to the gut.

She looked down. "But the truth is, my supposed intended and I agreed a long time ago that the match was never going to work. As a matter of fact, he is in love with someone else. We just haven't told our parents yet." She tried to get down from the table but he refused to let her.

"So you haven't agreed to this marriage."

She shook her head. "No."

Relief washed though him. From the moment he met her, she had struck him as being an independent thinker. It was no wonder that she resisted it. And if the man in question was indeed in love with someone else, it made things even easier.

"Good. Then there is no reason I can't do this." He yanked the sheet from her grasp and pulled her in for a punishing kiss.

She only hesitated a second before wrapping her arms around his neck and returning his kiss. She was like a drug in his system. Ever since he left her bed the previous night, he craved her taste, her scent, and the way she felt pressed against him.

Every part of her was perfection. Her skin felt like silk and the oil Connor had used on her only heightened its softness.

He needed her. Now.

He wanted to mark her in some way as his before anyone else came between them. But that wasn't right. Or fair to her. So he ruthlessly pushed his darker side to the back of his mind.

"Stand up." His voice came out rougher than intended, but she complied.

Her trusting, passion laden eyes soothed him more than any words she could have spoken.

"Turn around and put your hands on the bench."

Once again she did has he ordered, without question.

He ran his hand down her back. The span of his fingers very nearly covered the width of her narrow frame. When he reached her backside, he squeezed the rounded curve, before slipping his fingers between her legs. Her arousal coated his fingers, allowing him to slide easily between her folds. He found her clit and applied slow stead pressure. With his free hand he reached to her front and fondled her breasts.

He stroked and petted her until she panted and pushed against his hands, silently begging him for more. In a matter of seconds, he unfastened his belt and trousers and freed his erection.

"Bend over just a bit, beautiful. But keep your hands on the bench." When she did as he asked, he guided his cock to her entrance. With one quick thrust he was embedded in her silken heat. She gasped at the invasion but then pushed back, rubbing against him.

He released his hold of her breast and gripped her hips. He rolled his spine so that he pumped in and out of her in a steady rhythm. The pleasure intensified quickly making him wonder if he wasn't sensing hers through their connection.

They might not be mated, but the connection was there. They would only have to acknowledge it and accept it for it to snap into place.

But not yet. There were too many things for them to work out.

He reached around to her clit and pressed on her swollen bud. She whimpered with need, arcing her back trying to find her pleasure. Finally she stiffened then let out a hoarse cry as she climaxed.

Her tight channel spasmed around his cock, gripping him tightly, as his own release burst through him.

His fangs elongated. The urge to take her blood rode him. He tipped his head back in resistance. The last thing he wanted to do was to scare her. He had promised her that he didn't need to bite her. He would keep that promise even if it killed him.

"Oh, my," she panted.

He had no words for what he felt at that moment. Reluctantly he withdrew from her body then helped her stand upright.

As she turned to faced him, he drew his pants up and fastened them.

Her lips twitched into a grin. "Well...that's not quite how I expected my spa appointment to go, but I'm not going to complain."

"I am."

Her smile faltered until he added, "It's only been thirty seconds and I already want you again." He slipped his fingers into her hair. "What have you done to me?"

She wrapped her hand around his wrist. "Nothing you haven't

done to me." She closed her eyes and took a deep breath. "I don't understand this attraction. It's so strong and moving so fast that it's a little overwhelming." She held his gaze. "But I cannot deny it."

"Neither can I."

He kissed her, this time tenderly. When he drew back he told her, "Get your things. I'll walk you back to your room. Then I'll see what I can do about finding this person—this fae—you've been looking for."

21

REAGHAN checked each of the name plates posted outside the meeting rooms looking for the one Amarande had asked her to come to. She couldn't believe he had been willing to help her fulfil her mission.

She spotted him before she found the room.

Her heart skipped a beat when their gazes met. "You really think you found who I needed to talk to?"

He shrugged. "Maybe. You do realize that I am going out on a limb for you, right? Just remember, you promised that you only wanted to talk to her."

"And I meant it."

Amarande opened the conference room door and gestured for her to enter ahead of him.

The young man she had seen with Eirin looked up from where he sat at the table. He wore a gravely serious expression on his face. He glanced at Amarande then gestured to whoever waited off to the right to join him.

Reaghan stepped further into the room and looked to where the young man had motioned.

Eirin's eyes widened in fear and she let out a gasp. "No!" She tried to rush past the young man but he kept his hold of her hand. He looked at Amarande, obviously torn with indecision.

Amarande frowned.

Reaghan called out, "Eirin, please. I only wish to speak to you."

Tears pooled in Eirin's eyes and she struggled against the young man's hold on her. "No. I'm not going with you."

"What's going on here?" The young man asked. "You said your friend only wanted to talk to us."

"I'm not here to take you anywhere that you do not want to go." Reaghan tried to reassure her.

"I don't believe you." Eirin continued to try to get away. "My father sent you, didn't he?"

"No," Reagan told her. "He didn't."

"Then why are you here?" Eirin cried.

Reaghan glanced behind them at the open door. With a flick of her wrist, she closed it before answering. "The queen sent me."

Eirin stiffened. "The queen?"

"Yes. I was sent to ascertain how you fared." Reaghan swiveled around and faced Amarande and the young man. "Would you two excuse us? I need to speak to Eirin alone." Without waiting for their consent, she took Eirin's hand and conjured a bubble around the two of them so that no one could hear what they were saying.

"Please, you have to let me go," Eirin cried, even more panicked now. "I can't go back. I won't."

Reaghan grabbed Eirin by both arms. "Why can't you return? Tell me what has happened to you." She pushed just enough command into her words to force the girl's submission without influencing her.

Eirin shook her head. "You don't understand. I belong here now. With Jacob."

"Who is Jacob?"

"My mate," Eirin declared pointing to the young man who was beating on the bubble.

"You've mated with him?"

Tears rolled down the girl's cheeks as she nodded.

"Who forced you into the mating?"

The girl blinked in confusion. "No one forced me to do anything." She narrowed her gaze at Reaghan. "At least not yet."

"So you aren't being held here against your will?"

Eirin reared back in surprise. "No. Of course not. Why would you think that?"

"Because that is exactly what your father has told the king."

Eirin closed her eyes and shook her head. "Of course he did."

Reality set in. "He lied, didn't he?" Reaghan asked.

"Yes." Eirin angrily wiped her tears from her cheeks.

"You were never in danger. You were never kidnapped. And you were never held against your will, were you?"

"No. Of course not." Eirin shook her head. "I have always been a disappointment to him. No matter how hard I tried, I could never please him. Why can't he just accept that I'm not like everyone else? I have never felt like I belonged in the fae realm." She glanced at Jacob. "The first time I truly felt at peace was when I met Jacob."

"You love him." Reaghan had no doubt about the girl's feelings. She didn't even need to ask.

"I do." The tension drained from Eirin's slight form. "I had always heard the word but no one could ever explain it to me. But after meeting Jacob, I realize that you can't pinpoint it exactly. It's something you have to experience for yourself. Something you feel." She touched her own chest. "Here."

Reaghan nodded her understanding. "How do I know you aren't under some kind of enthrallment?"

"Jacob would never do that to me."

"How do you know?"

"I just know."

Even though Reaghan didn't believe it either, she needed to be able to convince others. "Then you won't object if I touched your mind to make sure?"

"Go ahead. I have nothing to hide."

Reaghan placed her thumb on Eirin's forehead and spread her other fingers along the side of her head above the ear. She looked deep into her eyes and used her senses to search for any kind of spell work or enthrallment. It only took a moment to verify there was nothing of the sort. She took a step back and let her hand drop. "It is as you say."

Eirin looked at her as if to say "I told you so."

After taking a deep breath Reaghan said, "For the sake of formality, I have to ask you three questions."

"Okay."

"And I'd like to record your responses so that the queen has indisputable proof. Your father has petitioned the Council to wage war upon the vampires for what they supposedly did to you. If I don't get word to the queen tonight, there is no telling what will become of the peace agreement between the realms."

Stony flints glittered in Eirin's eyes. "My father lied. And I will not be the means for him to wage war on people who have done nothing to deserve it. So, yes, I'll agree."

The girl's determination and moral compass were impressive. Especially for someone so young.

Reaghan took off the necklace she wore around her neck. She placed the crystal disc in her open palm and conjured a communication bubble. "Eirin, Daughter of Sativola, are you currently under the influence of anyone or anything or likewise being held against your will here in the mortal plane?"

Eirin directed her responses into the bubble. "No, I am not."

"And are you aware that if you remain here for an extended period of time the gateway to Eolande will close to you, your fae powers will fade, and your memories of the fae will dissolve like foam on the shore? Your lifespan shall be as limited as any human in the mortal realm."

"I am aware."

"And are you consciously choosing to remain in the mortal realm for the remainder of your life without access to your family, king, or queen?"

"I am." Eirin responded without the slightest hint of hesitation.

"So be it." The bubble in Reaghan's palm spun, glowing brighter with each turn until it burst and a shower of stardust fell to the ground.

Eirin looked up at Reaghan. "So now what?"

"Now you are free to be with your mate."

"You aren't going to stop me?"

Reaghan didn't blame the young woman for her doubt. "Why would I do that?"

"Because my father doesn't want me to stay here."

Folding her hands in front of her, Reaghan calmly explained, "You are of age. Your father has no say in your decision. He will be informed of your choice shortly."

Eirin's face fell. "He'll come for me."

"No, he will not."

"How can you be sure?"

"Because he made false claims to the king and to the elders and demanded justice for something he had no right to. There will be punishment for that."

"But he is an Elder."

"Exactly why there will be punishment. The queen had to become involved because the council was divided." Reaghan shrugged. "I was her solution to remedy the issue."

"That is it then?"

Reaghan smiled. "That is it."

Eirin still looked confused.

"The queen does not wish to make your choices for you, Eirin. She only wanted the truth."

Finally, the girl smiled. "Thank you."

"You're welcome."

"I can't wait to tell Jacob." Her smile faltered. "We were worried that we would have to move to prevent my father from finding us. Do we need to worry that there might be war?"

"I don't believe so. Your testimony is the proof we needed. And now that we know your father fabricated everything, I imagine the investigation will take a whole new direction."

The pounding on the bubble drew their attention. Reaghan gestured to the entry way. "I guess I should let your mate in before he hits one of my wards."

Eirin cringed and she gestured for him to stop. Amarande and Jacob were both scowling when Reaghan dissolved the barrier and let them pass. Eirin rushed into her mate's arms.

"My apologies for the abrupt separation but I had a delicate matter to discuss with Eirin." She gestured to the pair. "Perhaps introductions are in order?" Reaghan asked with a pointed glance at Jacob.

"Oh. Yes, of course." Eirin took a step forward and curtsied. "Mistress Reaghan, I present my mate, Jacob William Greenwood. Lord Greenwood's eldest son." Eirin's expression softened further when she looked at Jacob. "Jacob this is Mistress Reaghan of Owin, of the First Royal Family."

Amarande made a choking noise but she refused to look his way. She would have to deal with his surprise at learning her status later.

Jacob dipped his head in acknowledgement. "I am unsure if I should bow or not."

"No. Not at all." Reaghan moved toward them and extended her hand. "I am pleased to meet you Jacob Greenwood." She smiled. "Congratulations on finding each other. Go mbeidh grá agat nach gcríochnaídh riamh." *May you have a love that never ends.* She kissed them both on the cheek.

Eirin teared up again. "Thank you, Mistress."

"Now, go." Reaghan shooed them toward the door. "I have unfinished business with the grumpy one in the corner before I return home."

Jacob's eyes widened in surprise while Eirin smothered a giggle as they hurried to the door. Before they rushed away, Eirin paused and looked back. "Oh, and Mistress Reaghan, If you ever find yourself in the human realm again, you would be welcome in our home."

Reaghan smiled. "Thank you."

Once the door closed with a click, Reaghan took a deep breath and faced Amarande. His arms were folded in front of his chest, but she couldn't read his expression. She was emotionally worn out and all she really wanted to do was to crawl into bed with him and forget her obligations.

Based on the scowl he wore, she doubted that would even be an option.

22

AMARANDE waited until Eirin and Jacob had left to say anything to Reaghan. "What was that all about?"

He didn't care if he sounded angry. He was.

Reaghan took a deep breath. "Which part?"

"All of it."

She flicked her finger at the door, closing it. He still had trouble adjusting to the idea that she had magical abilities.

"So I take it Eirin was the person you were looking for?" he asked.

"Yes." She smiled. "Thank you. I do appreciate your help finding her. You have no idea how important that was."

"I would if you would tell me."

"I wish I could." She reached for his hand. "I really do."

He squeezed her hand in return. She was probably doing as she was commanded. No one understood following orders more than him. Didn't mean he had to like it. Especially if it impacted him or his people. "What was that thing you did with your necklace?"

She pulled the pendant from beneath her gown where he could see it. "This?"

"Yes. That."

"It's a memory sphere. It can recall specific memories a person wants to preserve." She tucked it under her shirt again. "I asked Eirin three very specific questions and I wanted to be able to replay it in Eirin's own words in case I am questioned or doubted when I return."

"What did you ask her?"

"I asked if she was being held against her will or presently under anyone's influence, if she was consciously choosing to remain in the human realm, and if she was aware that she would eventually lose her fae powers, leaving her with a mortal's life span."

He frowned. "It is that true? If she stays here, she becomes mortal?"

"Yes."

"That seems cruel considering she will be mated to a vampire. She will likely die well before him."

"I don't make the rules. It's the natural order of things. We fae cannot live outside of the fae realm without consequences. If we are separated from our world for long periods of time, our energy, our power, fades. Along with our memories of the fae world." She shrugged. "Granted, it takes longer than a normal human life span but it does happen."

"And she was fine with that?"

Reaghan nodded. "Yes. She said Jacob was her mate, her One. She was perfectly content to give up her life as a fae to be with him."

"Could he change her? Make her vampire?"

"In truth, I do not know. I've never heard of a fae being turned into vampire. Much less a fae, turning human, then turning vampire." She shook her head. "It's simply unheard of."

Her immortality was a lot to give up. Much less her family and way of life. But then…what would he give up for his own heartmate?

"Isn't she a little young to be making decisions like that?" he asked.

"Part of me wondered that as well. But no. She is of age. And she has very strong feelings about it. And for Jacob. That is obvious." She smiled. "I believe they will do well. I have faith."

He paced away before he did something ridiculous like kiss her and swear that they should be together as well. He looked back at her. "First Royal Family, huh?"

She grimaced. "Yes."

"I guess that partially explains why your parents were pushing your engagement?"

"Yes." She lifted her chin. "It was a political match that our fathers wanted."

"But not you."

She shook her head. "Pryderi didn't want it either."

"Pryderi. That's his name?" He tried to not growl at her, but wasn't sure he succeeded.

She nodded sadly.

"You have no feelings for him?"

She met his gaze. "Only as a friend."

Her answer partially soothed him. "If you don't want him, what do you want?"

Hope, worry, then disappointment flashed through her eyes. "I have long suspected what I want and what I can have are worlds apart." She shrugged. "But it doesn't really matter. My priority has to be getting this information to my queen."

"Why? How can whatever one girl had to say be so important?" Frustration clawed at him again. "I don't understand."

"I know you don't and I'm sorry. Suffice to say that power hungry men often twist things out of proportion when it serves their purposes."

"That seems to be true across all species." He reached for her hand. "Will you return?"

She sighed. "I don't know. A lot depends on what happens when I return."

"With the information you obtained?" He pointed to the necklace she wore around her neck. "Or with your family and Pryderi?"

"The information." She sighed. "Maybe both."

He tugged her closer. "Will you tell me if you do return?"

"Are you sure you want me to?" The vulnerability in her question slayed him.

"Very much."

"But I thought you were looking for a mate?"

"And I believe I found her." With his free hand he touched her hair. "But it seems the timing isn't quite right."

"Do you think there will ever be a time that is right?"

"Yes, I do." He had to believe it. Otherwise the darkness might overtake him.

His answer seemed to please her. Then her expression turned pensive. "We were always taught that a vampire can track you if they drink of your blood. Is that true?"

Her question took him by surprise. "Partially. Mated vampires can always find their partner. Many blood partners, as well. But it has more to do with their connection than the blood. Sex can also forge a bond, although not as easily as sharing blood. When couples take blood during sex, I've been told it's even more powerful."

"Then do it."

He drew back even as his fangs tickled his gums, signaling they were descending. She had no idea how much he wanted to sink this teeth into her flesh. To get lost in her body and her essence. But doubt lingered. She couldn't know what she was suggesting. "Do you think that is wise?"

"I strongly suspect that nothing I'm feeling where you're concerned is wise." She moved closer. "But I'm old enough to know that sometimes it's best to not question the opportunities fate drops into our laps. I don't know what will happen when I return home, but I don't want to regret having missed this moment with you."

He slid his fingers through her hair and cupped his hand around her neck so he could pull her closer. When their lips were only a breath apart he whispered, "Then perhaps you should lock the door."

She smiled and snapped her fingers. "Done."

Ruthlessly pushing aside all thoughts he may never see her again, he kissed her. Deeply, passionately. Everything that was in his cold, dead heart, he put into that kiss. Yet it still wasn't enough.

Without breaking their kiss, he backed her up to the table and lifted her so that she sat on the edge. She spread her knees, drawing him closer. They pushed at each other's clothing. Buttons were loosened and buckles unfastened. They each tried to do everything they could to remove all barriers between them. Finally she made all of their clothing vanish in a blink.

"That's a handy trick," he mumbled when he realized what she had done.

She giggled and pulled him in for another scorching kiss. Her legs wrapped around his hips, cradling him against her core.

He leaned on the table with one hand as he skimmed his fingers up her side with the other.

He brushed his lips across her cheek to the delicate curve of her ear so he could nuzzle that tender spot where the ear and neck met. Then he made his way downward. The sound of her heart beating against the thin layer of skin on her neck drew him like a magnet. His teeth lengthened when he recalled the coppery tang of her blood on his tongue but he refused to let it distract him from his destination.

As licked a path down her breast and belly, his senses were filled with a soft floral scent he now associated with her. Her fingers speared into his hair as he lowered his lips to the juncture between her thighs and licked her folds. Back and forth. Up and down, he worked her sensitive nub. When he sensed she was close, he slipped a finger into her channel. She rocked against his mouth then threw her head back with a wail. Her legs shook as her orgasm swept her away.

He stood then pulled her back to the edge of the table. With her cheeks flushed and her eyes glazed with passion, she was a breathtaking sight. "Wrap your legs around me, beautiful." As she complied, he guided his cock to her opening.

Slowly he pushed into her heat. When he was fully seated inside of her, he captured her lips. He gripped her hips, perhaps harder than he meant to but it was all he could do to stop himself from coming right then.

"Don't stop," she pleaded as her nails scraped his back. "Please."

He gritted his teeth fighting against the rising tide of his own pleasure. He rocked his hips back, slowly, even as she tried to pull him back in. But the quivering walls of her channel snapped the last thread of his control.

With a growl he began pumping in and out of her willing body in a steady rhythm. She arched her back, meeting his thrusts, seemingly relishing them. Almost mercilessly, he pounded into her seeking that pinnacle for them both. As he sensed it drawing near, he thrust his hand into her hair. Using a handful of her hair as leverage, he tilted her head back. Her breath came is short gasps. He leaned forward and ran his tongue over her collar bone and up the side of her neck.

She stiffened, then cried out with her second release.

Unable to hold out any longer, he slammed into her one last time. At the same time, he sank his teeth into the flesh of her neck.

As soon as her blood touched his lips, his ears began to ring with a high-pitched sound. His vision dimmed until all he could see were the images that assaulted him like a photo album in a hurricane. He clung to Reaghan as the storm raged. Then, for the first time in almost four hundred years, he felt a rush of warmth throughout his body.

Their mating had begun. His head spun but he fought the urge to seek that connection they shared. If he did, and if she returned it, their mating would be complete. He couldn't do that to her.

He wouldn't bind her to him and put her in a position where she might have to give up her world. Nor would he ask her to give up her powers and live a mortal life. Even if it meant living the rest of his life alone.

Without releasing his hold of her body, he pulled his mouth away from the temptation of her throat. He took several steadying breaths and focused his thoughts on where they were and what was happening around them.

Noises in the hallway, reminded him they were not really and truly alone.

"I don't suppose you thought to soundproof the room when you locked the doors, did you?" he asked.

She chuckled. "Actually, yes, I did."

"Good."

Despite his own fatigue, he helped her to sit up. Once again he was struck by how beautiful she was. "I thought all fae used a spell to hide their beauty from humans. Why didn't you?"

She blinked. "I did."

He drew back in surprise. "You did? Well you didn't cover much then because I still think you're absolutely beautiful." He kissed her even though her expression indicated she didn't really believe what he was saying.

"Would you like to see me without the glamour?"

"Yes, actually, I would." He held up one finger. "Although, first, would you mind terribly at least summoning my pants back in case someone knocks on the door?"

She smirked. "Of course."

His pants reappeared along with the rest of his clothes. "Not that I mind being naked with you. But I'd rather not have to explain where my clothes went if someone demanded to be let in."

"I suppose that would be hard to explain." She made her own clothes reappear also. "Okay, so this is me with glamour in place. This..." She waved her hand in front of her own face. "Is me without a glamour."

Amarande squinted at the brightening of her appearance. "Other than that glow around you, I don't see a difference."

Her mouth fell open. "You don't?"

"No." He ran his finger across her cheek. "I think you're beautiful either way."

"That can't be right." She bit her lip.

"Maybe it's because I have had so many dealings with non-human races that I've become used to those different brands of magic." He leaned in and kissed her one more time. "Or maybe I'm just so smitten with you that it doesn't matter what you look like on the outside."

She wrapped her arms around his neck. "I rather like that explanation."

A knock on the door interrupted their kiss. He rested his forehead against hers. "I figured someone would need this room before long."

She smiled sadly. "I need to go anyway. I must let the queen know I have the information."

"That means you'll be leaving."

"Yes."

A knot formed in his chest. "I hope that resolves whatever problem your queen has."

"I hope so too."

Whoever was at the door knocked again more insistently.

"I better go," she whispered.

He nodded.

In a blink she popped out of the room using her magic. The door locks clicked when they were released and Lord Bromwell poked his head in the door.

"Amarande," Lord Bromwell seemed surprised to see him. "Everything all right?" He glanced about the room.

"Yes." Amarande pasted a neutral expression on his face. "I take it you have this room next?"

"We do."

"Then I'll leave you to it." With a dip of his head, Amarande strolled out the door as if his world had not been shaken or that his cold, dead heart didn't ache.

 23

REAGHAN reappeared in her hotel room. With a sigh, she set her things on the end of the couch as she passed. She paused half way into the room and used her senses to search the space. Something was off. She slowly turned in a circle, inspecting her wards as well as the physical space. Nothing looked out of place but one of her wards pulsed with a strange orange glow.

She approached that one ward to take a closer look. It wasn't broken. Perhaps someone tried to get in and was stopped? She'd never seen one glow like that before. Caoilfhinn or Pwyll would know what it meant. She'd ask one of them about it later.

Right now she just wanted to crawl into bed and pull the covers over her head. But there wasn't time for that. Instead, she kicked her shoes off in the bedroom then headed to the bar.

She'd just said good-bye to the man who was very likely her One. Well… sort of said good bye. She'd taken the coward's way out and left without actually saying the words. She just couldn't bring herself to say it.

She needed a drink.

On the corner of the bar she found a bottle of wine – one of her favorite labels as well as a tray of Irish shortbread cookies. Another of her favorite treats.

She frowned. But where did they come from?

She snagged the card that had been left with the plate and read its contents. "Thank you."

Perhaps Lord Edrom had sent it. The script appeared to be masculine.

That could also be why the ward looked funny. It may have accepted the presence of one of the hotel staff in her room. It was a lovely gesture.

She opened the wine, the human way, using one of the stoppers from the bar then poured a healthy splash into a glass. She took the glass and a couple of cookies to the sofa.

Was Amarande really her One? The notion that he could be had flitted through her mind multiple times over the weekend. The fact that he had seen her true form, despite her glamour hinted that he was. She took a long drink from her glass. Actually, he'd even seen through the Queen's boosting of her glamour. Perhaps he really was her One.

Not that it impacted what she had to do. The information about Eirin had to reach the queen.

But what would happen after?

She had come to care for Amarande. That much she was certain of. And he seemed to care for her as well. Unless she was mistaken, he had hinted that she could be his mate. Or had that simply been because of the sex. The world shattering, amazing sex.

She sighed, wistfully, and took another drink.

Would she ever see him again? This weekend proved she was ready to return to the queen's service. Her mother wouldn't be pleased, but that wasn't her decision.

As a Queen's Agent, she could request assignments that sent her into the human realm, increasing the likely hood of seeing Amarande again. As far as she was concerned, that would be ideal.

She lifted the glass to take another sip and paused. Something was wrong. Her thoughts had become becoming disjointed and her vision had blurred a bit.

She tentatively smelled what was left in the glass. The faint aroma of moss and spice were just discernable over the acidic wine. She dropped the glass and hurried to the bar. There was nothing suspicious about the bottle itself. But when she sniffed the open bottle she instantly jerked away.

Her head began to swim.

Someone had laced the wine with casolea.

Casolea was an extremely rare plant. While beautiful when in full bloom, it had been outlawed in Eolande because of its toxic properties. There were only a two in all of Eolande allowed to grow them.

Which meant someone was trying to kill her. Someone from Eolande. They must have learned she came looking for Eirin. She needed to warn the queen.

As she staggered to the bedroom, her feet felt as if they were encased in heavy stone. Her vision wavered.

Amarande.

My queen.

Her shoulder hit the wall as she toppled sideways.

Must warn her.

Her heartbeat pounded in her head and spots danced across her eyes.

Amarande.

She fell to her knees as her body began to tremble.

Amarande. She pushed every bit of strength and focus she could manage into calling out to him. If he truly was her One, he would feel her distress call. He was likely her only hope.

Help me.

Then the darkness took her.

***

Amarande's head snapped up. He scanned the room.

"What's wrong?" Edrigu asked.

"Did you hear someone call my name?" Amarande asked.

Edrigu's brows rose in question. "No."

"Something is wrong." Amarande leapt to his feet, knocking his chair over in the process.

"What—"

Amarande ran out of the room with no explanation or excuse. That was Reaghan's voice he heard in his head. He didn't even question how he knew it or whether or not he was losing his mind. He only knew he needed to find her. Immediately.

But where would she be? Had she left for her home already?

He dashed from the meeting room, very nearly running over a couple of people along the way. He mumbled an apology but hurried on his way.

Her room was the only sure place he knew to check.

Panic threated to overtake him as he ran as fast as he could to the main staircase. He didn't bother with the lift just sailed up the multiple flights of stairs. As soon as he reached her floor, an overwhelming sense of dread filled him. He didn't even bother knocking. Instead, he slammed his shoulder against the door and muscled his way inside despite the burning sensation he felt.

"Reaghan?" He called out for her even as he searched the sitting room. When she didn't respond he headed to the bedroom.

If his heart had been beating it would have stopped when he found her laying in a heap on the floor.

He rolled her over. "Reaghan?" He touched her neck. Her pulse was weak.

"Reaghan!" He patted her cheeks, but she didn't respond.

He shouted out every bit of his frustration and despair. "No!"

He scooped her up and carried her to the hotel phone and dialed for the operator.

"How may I—"

"I need medical assistance in Miss McCarthy's room immediately! I don't know what is wrong with her. She's unconscious."

"Yes, sir. Right away. Do you wish for me to stay on the line?"

"I don't care! Just get someone up here now!"

"Yes, of course."

Amarande let the phone drop onto the floor next to him without bothering to disconnect the call. "Reaghan? Can you hear me? I need you to wake up." He lifted one of her eye lids up to check her pupils. They were dilated and her eyes were completely unfocused.

He pushed her hair aside and checked her neck for fresh bite marks or other injuries. Other than where he had bitten her earlier, he saw nothing to give any clue as to why she was unconscious.

"Hello? We had a call that someone might be injured?" A woman called from the sitting room. It was likely someone sent by the hotel, but he still went on the defense.

"In here," Amarande answered.

A woman with red hair swept into the room. Callum followed closely behind her.

Amarande's eyes narrowed in warning.

"My name is Riona. I'm the local healer." She knelt beside them. "May I take a look?" She gestured at Reaghan.

Amarande reluctantly shifted to one side so she could check her.

"Was this from you?" Riona pointed to Reaghan's neck.

"Yes. From earlier. But she was fine after our..." He glanced between Riona and Callum. "After our coupling."

Riona nodded in understanding and continued her exam.

"So what happened to her?" Callum's gruff question twanged Amarande's nerve.

"I don't know."

"What do you mean, you don't know?"

Amarande hissed in warning. "I. Don't. Know. I just found her. She was unconscious when I got here."

"Who kicked in the door?"

"Me." Amarande growled his answer, irritated by Callum's questions.

"Why?"

He patted Reaghan's hand and willed her to wake up. "Because I knew something was wrong and I needed to find her."

Callum folded his arms across his chest. "How did you know something was wrong?"

"She called for me."

From the corner of his eye he saw Callum pick up the handset that he'd carelessly dropped. "On the hotel phone?"

"No."

"Then how did—"

"She's my mate," he snapped. "I don't need a phone call to know when something is wrong."

"Something is wrong. Very, very wrong here." Riona looked up from examining Reaghan. "Without more information my guess is that she has been poisoned."

"Poison?" Amarande's chest grew tight. "Can you give her something to counteract it?"

"If I knew what she was poisoned with, maybe." Riona looked at Amarande. "I don't want to be an alarmist, but we need to get her to a hospital." She checked Reaghan's pulse. "I think her heart rate is slowing down."

"The closest one is more than an hour away," Callum pointed out. "Is there nothing you can do?"

"I can take educated guesses, but without confirmation of what she was poisoned with or is having a reaction to, that's all I can do."

"No." Amarande shook his head. "There has to be something you can do."

She waved her hand to them. "Look around. See if you can find any clues to what she might have triggered this."

Both men set to work looking around the bedroom and the sitting room.

"Other than a bite on her neck, I'm not seeing any external wounds or needle punctures so it may have been something she ingested."

"There's a glass of spilled wine behind the sofa," Amarande reported. He carefully picked up the glass, preserving the last few drops in the bottom.

"And an open bottle of wine on the bar." Callum added. "I'd be willing to bet they match."

Amarande sniffed the glass. It mostly smelled like wine, but there was a hint of some kind of herb also.

Callum did the same with the open bottle.

Both men frowned.

"Do you smell something funny?" Callum asked.

Amarande nodded and frowned harder. He handed the glass to Callum so he could verify if they were the same.

"I think that's what was in the glass." Callum took the bottle to Riona. "What do you make of this?"

She paused what she was doing and sniffed the open bottle. She too frowned. "What is that?"

"I'm not certain," Callum admitted. "It smells familiar but I can't quite place it."

"I don't recognize that scent at all. It smells almost floral, but not quite."

"Floral..." Callum returned the bottle to the bar but he looked as if he were thinking about something.

"Hey guys." Riona called out. "Why does it look as if she's changing?"

"She's fae." Amarande took Reaghan's hand as sparkles of light danced all over and around her body as the glamour faded away. Even though he knew she was fae and that they were capable of assuming alternate appearances, he hadn't thought about the fact that she may, in reality, look different.

"Oh my," Riona exclaimed. "I'd always heard the fae were stunningly beautiful creatures, but wow."

He glanced at Riona's awestruck expression. "Other than her hair being lighter, she looks the same to me."

Riona looked at him as if he had grown a second head.

"Fae. That's what it is," Callum exclaimed as he left the bar.

"What are you talking about?" Amarande asked.

"The smell. That's why it's familiar. It is a flower." Callum pointed at Riona acknowledging her earlier guess. "From Eolande."

"Where is that?" Riona asked.

"Where she's from." He tipped his head toward Reaghan. "The land of the fae."

"One of her own people poisoned her?" Riona asked.

"That would be my guess." Callum said grimly. "And if so, there won't be a lot we can do about it here." He looked at Amarande. "She needs to go home. Now. Her only chance may be finding someone there who can reverse the poison or give her an antidote."

"She said she was supposed to return tonight, sometime before dawn." Amarande replayed everything she had told him about her home over the weekend. "She said her queen tasked her with finding someone."

"The queen?" Callum asked.

"Yes."

"You're sure she said queen?"

"Yes. Why?"

Callum glanced at Riona. "I bet they used the portal."

Riona's eyes widened. "Do you think that's how she got here?"

"Possibly." Callum said.

"What portal?" Amarande asked. "What are you talking about?"

"I thought I sensed a disturbance." Riona looked to Amarande. "When did she arrive?"

"Thursday evening, I believe." The memory of first time he saw her was imprinted in his mind's eye. It looked as if she had just checked in at the hotel desk.

Riona nodded. "That's about when I sensed it." She looked to Callum. "You're probably right. But how do we get her home?"

"Someone will have to take her," Callum said matter-of-factly.

Amarande didn't hesitate. "I'll take her."

Riona and Callum both looked at him with a mixture of surprise and concern. "You do realize that Vampires are not exactly welcome in Eolande."

"Irrelevant," Amarande told him.

"As in, if you set foot on their side of the portal, it's extremely likely that you'll be killed." Callum stressed, "On sight."

Amarande looked down at Reaghan. "What other choice do we have?"

"None that I can see, if you want to save her." Riona shook her head. "I'm afraid this is beyond my ability to heal."

Amarande kissed the back of Reaghan's hand. If he didn't take Reaghan back to Eolande she would very likely die. But the price may be his own life.

She was his mate. It really wasn't a choice.

"So where is this damn portal and what do I need to do to get her through it?"

 24

REAGHAN wiped one hand across her face and struggled to open her eyes. The light coming through the windows was far too bright for her comfort but getting out of bed to close the curtains sounded as if it would require more energy than she had.

"Oh good. You're waking." A girl said from somewhere off to her right.

Reaghan turned toward the voice.

"You don't look so good, cousin."

There was only one person in the family with long brown hair like that. Lucille Klaire was the daughter of Reaghan's aunt. "Luci? Is that you?"

"Of course it is, silly." Her tone implied that Reaghan should have known that. Luci set her brush down and came to the bed. "Mother asked me to stay with you while she and Caoilfhinn went to address the council. I'm supposed to call for them when you wake."

Reaghan nodded, but the movement made her head hurt. "Where am I?"

"One of the guest rooms at the palace."

"How did I get here?" Her voice cracked making her realize just how dry her mouth was.

"I don't know exactly. I think one of the guards carried you in."

"But…" Reaghan sifted through her memories. Last thing she remembered was returning to her room at the hotel. "Oh no." She sat up suddenly which made her head swim. She pressed her palms to her temples to try to make it stop.

Tullamore.

Vampires.

The queen's mission.

"I need to find Caoilfhinn," Reaghan groaned even though the act of speaking made her head hurt worse.

"She and mother are at the gathering place." Luci looked worried. "They're trying to stop the angry people."

Reaghan rubbed her temples. "What angry people?"

"The ones trying to kill the vampire who tried to kill you."

Reaghan blinked in confusion. "The vampire who did what?"

Luci set her paintbrush on the tray below the paining she had been working on. "The vampire who brought you through the portal." She scrunched her nose. "I don't remember his name. All I know is that he was carrying you and we all thought you were dead." She grimaced. "Or nearly dead anyway. The king did something to separate you and the vampire so Queen Caoilfhinn could help you while he dealt with the vampire. But the vampire freaked out and kept trying to get to you and was yelling and stuff. He even beat up a couple of the king's guards before the king flashed him into a holding cell. It was cool!"

Following Luci's story made her head pound even worse. "Was the vampire's name Amarande?"

"Yes, something like that."

Reaghan turned so her feet dangled off the edge of the bed. She had to get to Amarande and the queen but standing didn't look like much of an option at that moment. If she did attempt to stand, she would most likely fall right to the floor.

"Mother said you're to remain in bed until the queen says you can get up," Luci scolded.

"Did she?"

"Yes." Luci bent in front of Reaghan and inspected her face. "I'm not sure it would be a good idea for you to get up either."

Reaghan snorted. "Do I look that bad?"

"I'm afraid so."

Reaghan smiled at Luci's no-nonsense answer. You could always trust her for an honest, yet candid answer.

"You said they went to the gathering place?" Reaghan asked.

"Yes."

Reaghan studied the painting Luci had been working on while she waited for her stomach and her head to settle a bit. It was a portrait of a man and woman standing in a doorway. Their backs faced the viewer so their faces couldn't be seen. But their arms were wrapped around each other and the couple looked out through some kind of opening. It almost looked like one of the portals used to go to the human realm.

The man had been painted with dark colors but the woman was portrayed in pale whites and blues. Yet the lighting surrounding them was the same for both of them. Without any shadows on either of them.

There was something eerily familiar about the couple.

"That is a very pretty painting. How long have you been working on it?" Reaghan asked.

"Not long." Luci used a rag and wiped off the ends of her brush then put it into her case. "I painted the background several days ago, but I didn't see the people until this morning."

"What did the people tell you when you finally saw them?"

"Nothing. They never say anything." Luci sounded a little sad. "I just see them. And feel what they're feeling."

"What are they feeling?" There was a part of Reaghan that was afraid of what Luci might tell her.

Luci considered her painting. "They love each other. A lot." Her blue eyes locked onto Reaghan. "But he's worried and afraid."

Reaghan's heart stuttered in her chest. "Of what?"

"That he's going to lose her. He knows he almost did."

The lump in her throat made it hard to swallow. "What about the woman?"

"She's afraid too." Luci's gaze turned distant. "Kind of the same thing but in a different way. I don't quite understand why or how."

"It's okay. I understand what she feels." Reaghan reached out to Luci. When she came to the edge of the bed, Reaghan intertwined her fingers with Luci's and brought their joined hands to her cheek. "Thank you," she whispered.

"For what?"

Reaghan forced a smile even though her head pounded and fear for Amarande weighed on her heart. "For staying with me while I slept."

"Mother says you were poisoned."

Having her suspicions verbalized made Reaghan cringe. "I suspect that as well, but I don't know for sure."

"Mother thinks you were. She and the queen are trying to figure out who did it. Caoilfhinn is quite cross."

An angry queen was no small matter. Hopefully none of that

anger would be aimed at Amarande. She groaned and touched her head. "My head is killing me."

Luci scrunched her nose. "Why don't you make it stop?"

"I tried, but I don't think it did anything. It feels like my powers are drained."

"Mother could fix it." Luci grimaced. "I would offer to try but I don't really know how yet."

She squeezed Luci's hand. "It's ok. I don't suppose you could help me get to the gathering place, could you? I'm not sure I could flash anywhere right now with any accuracy."

"Mother said to let her know when you woke up." Luci bit her lip and considered Reaghan. "I suppose it could be considered the same thing if I took you there, right?"

"I don't want you to get into any trouble, but I have a really bad feeling that I need to help Amarande and I'm not sure I could get there in time if I walk."

"The vampire is your friend, right? He wasn't the one who hurt you."

"Yes. He is my friend." She glanced at the painting again. "He would never hurt me."

Luci nodded once, as if she had made up her mind. "Then yes, I'll help you." She faced Reaghan and grasped both of her hands. "Ready?"

"One thing." Reaghan squeezed Luci's hands to stop her.

Luci's brows rose in question.

"If there's trouble at the gathering place, promise me you will flash right back here so Aunt Birkita knows where to find you. Your mother would never forgive me if anything happened to you."

The little imp rolled her eyes. "I promise."

"Okay, then let's go find my vampire."

Luci nodded her head determinedly then closed her eyes and flashed them into the gathering place.

Reaghan had to hold onto Luci while she steadied herself.

"Are you okay?" Luci looked up at Reaghan with concern.

"Yes. Just a little weak." She looked around at the crowd that had assembled at the gathering place. "Do you see your mother or the queen?"

Luci kept her arm around Reaghan's waist as she pushed up on her toes to have a look. "No. But they're probably in the middle there."

"That's my guess as well." She gave Luci a squeeze. "Thank you for bringing me here but I'm not sure this is the best place for you. You'd probably be better off returning to the palace."

"Are you sure you'll be okay?"

"I have to be if I want to save Amarande, don't I?"

"You'll save him. You'll see." Luci gave her a quick kiss on the cheek then smiled up at Reaghan before flashing out.

Reaghan took a deep breath then pushed her way into the crowd. She ignored the gasps and whispers as the people she passed realized who she was. When she reached the center of the crowd, she very nearly fainted on the spot.

Amarande was chained to a tree in the center and a group of men, her father included, were shouting to the king to have him killed. Caoilfhinn and several other women, her Aunt Birkita included, were doing their best to calm the crowd.

Amarande's clothes were disheveled and ripped in several places. There was a fresh cut on his cheek that looked deep. His head hung low and his shoulders slumped as he had been defeated.

One of the men clustered near her father broke free of the group and rushed toward Amarande. A knife glinted in the sunlight as he raised it above his head.

"No!" Reaghan shouted as she directed every drop of energy she could muster at the assailant to knock him away from Amarande. She dropped to her knees, weakened by the effort.

Amarande's head jerked up. Their gazes locked onto each other. At first he looked as if he couldn't believe what he was seeing. Then his face hardened into sheer determination. He strained against his bonds trying to get free.

The crowd gasped.

Caoilfhinn and her aunt rushed to Reaghan's side but she never took her gaze off Amarande.

"Are you all right?" Caoilfhinn asked as she and Birkita helped Reaghan stand.

"Not really. Help me get to him. Please. He needs me."

"I don't think that's wise," Aunt Birkita said.

"Actually, that may be exactly what we need," Caoilfhinn countered.

Her father bristled at them. "Reaghan, what are you doing here? You very obviously should be in bed. We'll take care of this creature."

"Owin, if you're not going help then stand aside," Aunt Birkita told him.

"He's not a creature," Reaghan protested.

"He is vampire. He attacked you," her father said as if that explained everything.

"He did not attack me," Reaghan argued.

"What do you mean? Of course he did." He pointed at her. "The marks on your neck prove it."

Reaghan shook her head and prayed for strength and patience to do what she had to do.

When they reached Amarande, Caoilfhinn and Birkita steadied her until she could stand on her own.

"I know you want to go to your vampire, but give me a moment first," Caoilfhinn whispered in her ear.

Reaghan nodded she had heard her.

"My king," Caoilfhinn said to her husband. "I believe this would be an appropriate time to hear what Reaghan has to say on the matter. Don't you agree?"

"Yes," the King said. "I would be very interested in hearing what she has to say about this vampire." He placed himself between Amarande and the men who had been calling for his death. He gestured to Amarande. "Do you know him?"

"Yes, Your Majesty, I do," Reaghan answered.

"Was he in anyway responsible for your, as I understand, poisoning?" the king asked.

"No, Your Majesty. I have no reason to believe that he was." She looked at Amarande and allowed the love she felt for him to shine through. "He has never once given me a reason to believe that he would ever harm me."

"The girl is obviously enthralled, Your Majesty." Sativola, the head of one of the other royal families, pointed at Reaghan. "Surely you can see that."

Reaghan frowned at him. "Enthralled? By whom?"

"By the vampire," of course. "Owin, you see it, don't you?"

Reaghan looked at her father in confusion. He frowned as he assessed her.

"Oh, for pity's sake," Aunt Birkita spoke up. "Reaghan is not enthralled. Between the cleansing spells and the purifying herbs that the queen and I used to draw the poison out, a simple enthrallment would have been broken long ago."

Sativola pointed at Amarande. "He probably cast it again as soon as he saw her again. That's why she is trying to save him."

Reaghan narrowed her gaze at Sativola. "You realize I came to save him before I ever saw him again, don't you?"

"Enthrallment has been forbidden by vampire law for centuries," Amarande told them. "It's an act punishable by death."

"He lies," Sativola protested.

"Actually, he does not," Pwyll, Reaghan's brother said as he pushed his way to the front of the crowd. "I've studied their laws. Do you wish to dispute my knowledge on the subject?"

Reaghan smiled up at her older brother as he wrapped his arm around her shoulder and gave her a squeeze. "I'm glad you're up and about, sister." He dropped a kiss on top of her head then whispered, "You should probably introduce me to your vampire soon before he breaks through those chains and rips my arms off because he thinks I'm one of your suitors."

She glanced at Amarande. If looks could kill, Pwyll would have been dust at her feet.

Reaghan's heart warmed. If he became that jealous over her brother's actions, she must matter to him at least a little.

She just needed to get him free so she could find out how much.

 25

AMARANDE still couldn't believe that Reaghan was alive.

Throughout the endless questioning and torture he'd endured he had alternated between hope she still lived and despair he had not been fast enough and they had been unable to save her. When they dragged him from his holding cell and into the courtyard then chained him to the tree, shouting all the reasons why he should die, he mistakenly believed Reaghan had died. In that moment, despair won the battle. He didn't fight the men who had taken him, even though he likely could have taken on a least a couple of them. He might have even been able to fight his way free and find his way to the portal to go home.

But he realized, he didn't care.

Nothing matter if Reaghan was no longer in the world.

Even if they were never meant to be together, he didn't want to live in a world – either one—without her.

It wasn't until she broke through the crowd and saved him from what he expected to be a death blow, that his desire to live had been rekindled.

Now he needed to break free of whatever was holding him to the tree and make the newcomer get his hands off of Reaghan. Whoever he was, she obviously cared for him. She didn't protest at all when he embraced her. He glared at the man, as he struggled to find some weakness in his bonds.

He blinked in confusion as Reaghan waved to get his attention then mouthed something at him.

Brother.

The man with his arm around her shoulder was her brother? He studied the two of them side by side. Finally, he noticed the similarities in their features. Jealousy drained from him as if someone had pulled a plug. Perhaps he didn't need to maim the man after all.

"Please, Your Majesties," Reaghan pleaded. "Amarande had nothing to do with poisoning me. If anything, he saved my life." Her gaze landed on Amarande. He would have sworn there was affection in her eyes but that could have been hope on his part. "He has every reason to distrust our people, yet he risked his life to bring me home. All that this..." She made a sweeping gesture of the crowd of people around them. "...is doing is fostering the vampires' long held belief that the fae are dangerous, unpredictable, and not to be trusted. Is that really what we want?"

"I don't give a damn what any vampire thinks," Sativola spat. A couple of the other men with him made noises of agreement.

"I do," the king said with deadly calm.

The crowd let out a collective gasp. Sativola stepped back as if he had been slapped.

The queen went to stand beside her husband. Pride radiated from her as she looked up at him.

"For too long we have hidden on our side of the tentative truce with the vampires. I see no reason why we cannot bridge the gap between us. I suspect there is much we have lost by being at odds with each other. I should very much like to know if there are things we could learn from each other." The king's gaze traveled around the crowd. "Now. I believe we should move this discussion into the assembly room where perhaps calmer heads can prevail."

"There is nothing this vampire has to say that will dissuade me," Sativola said. "But if that is what our king desires then so be it."

"It is." The king snapped his fingers. In a blink, part of the group had been moved from the courtyard into a large room that looked like a cross between a library and courtroom. The ceiling was well over two stories high and made from colorful glass or crystal. White stone pillars supported the weight of the decorative ceiling and created a natural gathering place in the center of the oblong room. The floors were a polished stone that reminded him a bit of white marble, except for the iridescent flecks of color that twinkled and moved like falling stars, as if it had its own life force.

Amarande's stomach turned as his reality shifted from one place to the other. He was no longer chained to a tree, but his hands were still bound behind his back. How the fae did that popping in and out of places baffled him.

"Now that the crowd is no longer an issue, there are a few things I need answers to, including Reaghan's illness or poisoning or whatever befell her." The king looked at the queen. "Was she poisoned?"

"She was." The queen conjured an image of a flower Amarande had never seen before in the space above her palm. "Lady Birkita and I both believe it was casolea poisoning."

"Something not native to the human realm," the king said. "Which means someone from this realm was involved."

And with that one statement, Amarande transformed his despair and hopelessness into anger. Now he just needed to know his target.

"That is what we believe also," the queen said.

The king faced Amarande. "How did you know where the portal was to enter our realm?"

Amarande forced a neutral expression on his face. He wasn't going to expose anything. Not his feelings. And certainly not anyone in the human realm who helped him. "An associate of mine."

The king narrowed his gaze. "Who?"

Amarande shook his head. "That I will not share." He held the king's stare blocking out all thoughts except those of Reaghan and how he felt when he thought he was about to lose her. He'd always heard that some fae could read thoughts. If the king could, he wanted him to know he had been sincere about saving Reaghan.

"How do I know this…associate of yours isn't giving out the location to everyone he meets?"

"I admit that I don't know him well, but he is an honorable man. And unless you have had a rash of humans or vampires or others marching in and out of here, I doubt it is an issue. He only shared it with me after the Tullamore healer admitted that Reaghan's care was beyond her abilities and since Reaghan was fae, her best chance of surviving was to return home."

"He knew the witch?"

"Yes."

The king drew back. "Very well."

It appeared the king knew Riona. Made Amarande glad he mentioned her.

The queen stepped forward. "How did you and Reaghan meet?"

Amarande glanced at Reaghan. A smile flittered across her face. "Reaghan came to Tullamore as a guest violin player at a meeting I was attending this weekend. We met by chance one evening while she was practicing her violin."

"How was she invited to Tullamore in the first place?" the man Amarande believed to be Reaghan's father asked.

The queen spoke up. "That was my doing, Owin. I arranged for their guest musician to unexpectedly lose their voice so that Reaghan could go to the meeting and take care of something for me."

"Since I wasn't informed that my daughter would be sent on a royal errand to the human realm, I'm afraid I must ask what that errand was for," Owin said.

"I believe we have gotten off topic," the man with the long, pale white hair that the queen had called Sativola interjected. "I thought we were here to determine the fate of this..." He gestured in Amarande's direction. "...this creature."

Creature? Amarande pulled at his bonds.

"You're not curious why Reaghan was in the human realm?" The queen challenged Sativola.

"Not particularly," Sativola said.

Based on their expressions, more than one person in the room considered Sativola's behavior suspicious. At least it wasn't just him. There was something about the pale haired man that rubbed Amarande the wrong way. Something more than just his pompous attitude.

Owin moved closer to Reaghan. "Why were you in the human realm? And why were you consorting with a vampire?"

Reaghan looked at the queen. The queen nodded, as if giving her permission to answer. "I was asked to attend the event the vampires were having at Tullamore this weekend. Specifically, I was asked to locate Eirin, daughter of Sativola, and ascertain her situation and state of mind."

"And did you accomplish this?" One of the other women asked. "I did."

"And what did she—" The woman's question was cut off.

"How is any of this relevant?" Sativola asked. "The only thing that needs to be settled here is the fate of this vampire. If you believe he is not guilty of harming Reaghan then he should be returned to the mortal realm with his memories stripped."

Amarande balked at the idea of having his memories stripped. He didn't want to forget Reaghan or how they met or the first time they made love. Reaghan didn't seem any happier about the idea.

The pale haired man was seriously pissing him off now.

The queen frowned at Sativola. "It's relevant because I believe it's the reason that Reaghan was poisoned." The queen turned back to Reaghan and said, "Please tell us everything you saw and learned about Eirin and her situation. First, did you locate her at Tullamore?"

"I did. She was hard to find. When I finally did get to speak with her alone, she was extremely frightened," Reaghan told the group.

"Of what?" One of the other women in the room asked.

"She thought I was there to either kill her or drag her home."

"That is rubbish. You must have misunderstood her desire to come home," Owin denied.

"I know without a doubt she did not want to return." Reaghan smiled. "As a matter of fact, she was prepared to fight for her right to remain with her mate, as she called him."

"Her mate?" Reaghan's brother asked.

"Yes." She glanced at her brother. "As it turns out, she found her One. They love each other very much. And if what I observed of the two of them together—before she knew who I was—they are very much in love with each other."

"Are you sure she was not under some sort of spell or enthrallment?" The woman standing near the queen asked with a heavy dose of sarcasm and a pointed look at Sativola. Amarande liked her immediately.

"Not that I detected. I even made a few discreet inquiries about her mate while I was there. He seemed to be a respected member of their community. And he comes from a good family."

Obviously Reaghan had been busy. He was both proud of her and concerned no one picked up on what she had been doing. Including himself.

Sativola scoffed, earning him a hard look from not only the queen but a couple others.

"How can you be certain she answered your questions freely?" Owin asked.

"Because once I explained why I had come, and swore to her that I meant neither her nor her mate any harm, she calmed and willingly spoke to me. She even offered to let me link with her memories and see that she was there of her own free will." Reaghan lifted a crystal disc that hung from a gold chain around her neck from the folds of her dress. "This will prove that she is sincere in her desire to remain in the human world."

The queen squinted at the necklace. "Is that a memory sphere?"

"It is," Reaghan confirmed.

The queen nodded in approval. "Would you mind replaying whatever memory you have that is relevant for everyone?"

Reaghan held the crystal in her palm and closed her eyes. Images of Eirin when Reaghan had pulled the stunt with the bubble shield were projected just above Reaghan's palm for everyone to see. Amarande had to admit that was a handy device.

He hadn't realized Reaghan thought Eirin might be held against her will. But he had the benefit of knowing Jacob and his family. No wonder she had separated Eirin from them. He probably would have done the same thing.

When it finished playing, the queen directed her words at Sativola. "I believe I have seen all I needed to see or hear."

The king asked, "Does anyone here doubt the validity of this information?"

Amarande looked around the room. Most shook their heads no. Inwardly, he breathed a sigh of relief.

Sativola sniffed in disdain. "I suppose I have no alternative but to drop my petition to invade the human realm."

The king nodded once. "Does anyone have any other concerns they would like to address regarding Eirin?" He glanced about the room. "No? Since we have representation from each of the royal families then I will consider this matter closed and we will hear no more of it."

That was all it took to resolve something here? The vampire lords would have taken three days to debate every single detail. Perhaps having a king and queen in place wasn't a bad idea.

"Sativola, I wish to speak with you privately." The king added, "That is not a request."

"As you wish, my king." The words may have been said, but the warmth and sincerity were missing.

The queen held up one finger. "There is one more matter, my king."

"What's that my queen?"

"We need agreement on the fate of..." The queen looked his way. "How rude of us. I don't believe I asked for your name."

"Amarande." His voice cracked from lack of hydration.

The queen smiled. "Amarande. We need to determine what is to become of Amarande."

For a brief moment he thought he'd gotten lucky and they had forgotten about him. Guess it had been too much to hope for that they'd simply let him walk away.

Preferably with Reaghan.

 26

REAGHAN'S gut clenched. All she wanted to do was free Amarande and pretend that none of this had happened.

"While the question of punishment has been dismissed, I do believe we need to address what is to become of him." Caoilfhinn said, gesturing to Amarande. "I believe the options before us are that he should be escorted to the portal he entered through and returned to his own time and place with absolutely no repercussions, or that he have his memories wiped before being sent back through the portal, or that he be required to remain here in Eolande."

"You would allow a vampire to live in Eolande?" Sativola asked in outrage.

"Why not?" Caoilfhinn asked.

Reaghan's heart hammered in her chest. She studied Amarande's expression trying to get a sense of what he might be feeling but his I-don't-feel-anything mask was firmly in place.

"I am not sure it would be safe for him to remain in Eolande," Pwyll pointed out.

Reaghan reared back in surprise at her brother's comment. "Why do you say that?"

"Did you not see how everyone acted earlier? They were ready to kill him on the spot without council consent or even a hearing. Just because he was vampire they believed the worst of him."

Reaghan's heart sank. Pwyll was right. It would be dangerous. But she wasn't ready to give up all hope. "Even if he were accompanied by someone?"

"You mean a guard?" Pwyll asked.

Amarande frowned at that.

"No, an advocate. A partner, of sorts."

Amarande and her brother both seemed doubtful about her idea.

"And what would being a partner entail?" her father asked, equality as doubtful.

"Ensuring that he doesn't wander into areas where he might encounter unfriendly people. An advisor maybe on how things work in Eolande."

"An escort, then," Pwyll said.

"That's a good idea," Caoilfhinn beamed her approval. She looked at Reaghan. "And are you willing to accept responsibility for your vampire?"

Reaghan's father stepped in. "I don't think Reaghan would be the best choice. Assuming of course this is the option we agree to. Perhaps her brother would be better suited?"

"No one else." Reaghan said firmly. She looked at Caoilfhinn. "Yes, I am willing to do it." Her gaze drifted to Amarande. "If he wishes to stay. And if he accepts me."

"But what about Pryderi?" her father asked. "What will people think if you're seen wandering the streets with another man?"

It took all of Reaghan's discipline to not roll her eyes. "Father, you understand that Pryderi and I were never a good match, don't you? We tried to make it work in order to please you and his father, but if we move forward with a union, it will never make either of us happy."

"What are you saying?" Owin asked with a frown.

She lifted her chin. "That I do not love Pryderi. He is not my One. He never was." She swallowed the knot that had formed in her throat. "I love someone else."

"As do I."

Reaghan turned. "Pryderi." She smiled sadly as he approached.

Pryderi took Reaghan's hand and kissed her gently on the cheek. He squeezed her hand, silently offering his support.

"One of you needs to explain what is going on here," her father demanded.

"I whole heartedly agree," Pryderi's father said as he stepped forward.

"Actually, I believe we can all agree that this is not the time or place for this discussion. Suffice to say that Reaghan and I agreed long ago that we would never make each other happy except to remain as friends, we just hadn't bothered to tell anyone else."

"Well, I—"

Pryderi held up his hand, effectively cutting off his father. "We'll discuss it later. I only came to deliver pertinent information to the king." He gave Reaghan's hand one last squeeze then went to the king. He handed the monarch a scroll of paper and whispered something so only the king could hear.

"What's going on?" Reaghan's father asked.

"What is this all about?" Pryderi's father asked at the same time.

The king glanced at the contents of the scroll then looked up. "This…" He held up the paper. "Is proof that Sativola made arrangements with a known criminal to have casolea added to Reaghan's food or drink so in hopes that she wouldn't be able to return to Eolande with the information she collected about Eirin."

A gasp went around the room.

Sativola pointed at Pryderi. "That is a lie!"

"Pryderi, that is a serious charge," his father said.

"I know," Pryderi agreed. "But the evidence I collected is irrefutable."

Several council members looked at Sativola in shock.

"This is preposterous," Sativola protested. "I would never do such a thing."

The men argued about whatever was written on that scroll, but Reaghan's attention remained fixed on Amarande. His hands had balled into fists and he pulled at his restraints. His eyes slowly turned from blue to red. Lucky for Sativola his bonds held firm. She edged closer to Amarande while everyone else in the room was distracted by the new information.

If Amarande broke free, she felt certain he would kill Sativola. And then he would most certainly be put to death. She couldn't allow that.

"Amarande," she whispered his name, trying to breach the fury descending upon him. "Look at me."

Slowly his focus turned away from Sativola and onto to her. She held his gaze as she edged even closer. Blocking out the shouting and the noise around them, she focused only on him. Their connection snapped into place just as she reached him. "I'm fine. I'm here," She whispered. "Let the king and queen decide his punishment. If you do anything to him right now I won't get to see you again." She caressed his cheek. "And I very much want to see you again."

She pushed all of her feelings through their connection until the red faded from his eyes, indicating he was once again in control. "Are you okay?"

"Yes." He closed his eyes and rested his forehead against hers. "Thank you."

"You're welcome."

"Reaghan, what are you doing?" her father demanded from across the room.

"Only what I should be." She turned around in time to see Sativola conjure a curse and hurl it in their direction.

With a roar, Amarande broke free of his bonds. He wrapped his arms around her, twisted and took both of them to the ground. From the corner of her eye she saw Pwyll blast Sativola, knocking Sativola off balance. The curse or whatever Sativola had conjured bounced off the protection shield that only the queen could have conjured in such a short time.

Reaghan's breath was knocked from her chest when she and Amarande hit the ground. Amarande took the brunt of the fall but her ribs still ached from the impact. He clutched Reaghan to his chest as he searched the area around them. "Are you all right?" He finally asked.

She nodded, but couldn't find her voice just yet.

"Guards, take Sativola into custody. Now," the king demanded.

There was scuffling and shouting as the queen rushed to Reaghan and Amarande. "Are you all right?"

Reaghan lifted her head from Amarande's chest. "Yes, I think so." She looked up. "Amarande? Are you okay?"

He took several deep breaths through his nose then growled. "Yes." He rolled to one side and eyed the guards scuffling with Sativola. The amount of hatred in that glance could have burned a hole through the toughest metal.

She put her hand on his chest. "Later. Stay with me for now. Please?"

He tore his gaze away from the guards and focused on her. He nodded in agreement.

"Let me check you both," the queen said.

"I'm fine," Amarande assured her as he started to stand.

"I wasn't asking." With a simple look Caoilfhinn reminded him who the queen was.

Reaghan bit back her smile and submitted herself, and Amarande, to the queen's attentions.

"I don't think that curse got either of you," Caoilfhinn finally told them.

"Thanks to your protective shield?" Reaghan asked.

Caoilfhinn shrugged.

Reaghan touched Caoilfhinn's hand. "Thank you."

"It was the least I could do after everything you went through. For me. And for Eolande."

Reaghan took Amarande's hand and let him help her up.

Reaghan's father rushed toward them. "Are you all right?" He must have realized that Amarande was no longer bound for he stopped, a short distance from them and cast a leery glance his way.

"Yes, Father. We're both fine. Caoilfhinn deflected the curse he tried to hit us with."

Pwyll joined them. "Good thing. There is no telling what that old fool would have done to you two."

Reaghan wrapped her arm around Amarande's waist and pressed herself against his side. His arm naturally wrapped around her shoulders like a shawl of protection. She instantly felt better.

"Other than all the explosions, yelling, and screaming, how are you feeling, Reaghan?" Caoilfhinn asked. "You just rolled out of a sick bed. This excitement must be taking a toll on you."

Reaghan grimaced. "I am a little tired. But at least I forgot about my aching head while all the craziness was happening."

"That would be the after effects of the casolea. Here." Caoilfhinn placed her palm on Reaghan's forehead then cupped the back of Reaghan's head with her other hand and closed her eyes.

A stream of warmth washed the annoying throbbing pain from Reaghan's head. She sighed with relief. "Thank you. Again."

The queen nodded.

"You're going to need to drink lots of fluid to finish washing those poisons out," Birkita said as she joined their group.

"Yes, ma'am." Reaghan smiled at her aunt.

"Anything else she should be doing to ensure her recovery?" Amarande asked.

"Rest." The queen and Aunt Birkita said in unison, as if they both knew she would be hard pressed to remain still for long.

Pwyll snickered and looked away.

The king finally joined them. "Sativola is being escorted to the Ferrum Tower."

Reaghan's mouth fell open in surprise. She had not heard of the tower being used in centuries. It was used only for the most dangerous criminals.

"Are you worried that we cannot hold him?" Caoilfhinn asked as she slipped her hand around his elbow.

"A little." Lairgnen looked at Owin. "What do you think?"

Her father grimaced. "Sativola is powerful. And quite skilled with spells." He shook his head. "If he is as angry as he appeared, then yes, you probably will have a fight on your hands."

Lairgnen expression turned grim. "I was afraid of that."

"What will you do?" Owin asked what everyone was likely wondering.

"I'm afraid he will leave me no choice in the matter. If he refuses to stand before the council and face punishment for his actions, then he will die by my sword."

"I certainly hope Naois is ready to step up," Pwyll said.

"Actually, Gwynith is older than him by eight minutes," Owin told the group.

"Really?"

Reaghan was instantly suspicious of the speculative gleam in Pwyll eye. "You should probably steer clear of Gwynith."

"Why do you say that?" Pwyll asked.

"Because I know that look. It means you're about to do something really stupid even though you think it's smart." Reaghan told added, "And if it has anything to do with Gwynith, then be prepared to be bested."

"We'll see."

The queen clapped her hands together. "Well, this has been fun, but the King and I have business to attend to. Owin, would you please send word to Gwynith and Lavena about Sativola's detention. They likely already know, but a formal notice from a council member is warranted, I believe."

Owin nodded curtly. "Of course."

"Reaghan, you need to rest and heal." Caoilfhinn pointed at her. "Consider that a royal order."

The king extended his hand to Amarande who hesitated only a fraction before taking it. "I'm sorry our meeting was not under better conditions. If you wish to stay in Eolande, you are welcome. But if you wish to return to the human realm, you only need ask and a portal will be opened for you. We will leave that decision in your…" He glanced at Reaghan. "…and Reaghan's hands."

The queen embraced Reaghan and whispered. "Good luck."

"Thank you, my queen." Reaghan returned her embrace.

Caoilfhinn clasped Lairgnen's hand.

"Oh, and Amarande, tell Callum that I'll be popping in later." With one last pointed look at Amarande, the king and queen disappeared.

"I need to find Luci," Aunt Birkita said. "I assume she returned to the palace?"

"Yes. I made her swear that she would go back to the room where I woke," Reaghan assured her.

"Good." Aunt Birkita kissed Reaghan on the cheek. "I will reiterate what Caoilfhinn said. You need to rest." She looked up at Amarande. "Make sure she does."

"I will do my best," Amarande said.

"Thank you." She patted Amarande on the arm then she too disappeared.

"Can everyone do that?" Amarande asked Reaghan.

"Do what?"

"Disappear."

Reaghan smiled. "Only the royals have the ability.

"May I assume the two of you will be joining us at home?" Owin asked. "I believe we have things to discuss."

Reaghan looked up at Amarande, half dreading his answer.

"No, I think not."

Reaghan's heart sank. This was where she lost the man she loved. Loved?

When had that happened? She watched as Amarande talked with her father and brother, but she didn't hear a word they said. Her gut screamed he was her One but her mind stumbled over the fact that they had met only a few human days ago. She paused in order to listen to her heart. It whispered truth. It said never let him go.

27

"**I** believe Reaghan and I need to talk," Amarande told Reaghan's father.

Owin pressed his lips together. He obviously didn't like Amarande's answer but he finally gave a brisk nod. "Very well. I hope you will come to the house when you have worked things out."

Pwyll stepped forward. "You two are welcome to use my place if you want some privacy." He shot a pointed look at Amarande. "To talk. I have palace business to take care of then I'll likely check in with father at the house after."

"Thank you." Amarande extended his hand.

Pwyll shook with him, the way humans do. "Be good to my sister so I don't have to smash your face in."

"That won't be an issue," Amarande assured him.

"Are you strong enough to pop over to my place?" Pwyll asked Reaghan. "You look a little pale."

"I could probably manage were it just me. But I don't think I can handle both of us. We can walk," Reaghan said. "It's not far."

"Are you sure?" Pwyll asked. "I could always take him."

"I'm not sure about this disappearing business so I'm fine with walking. Unless that will tire you out." Amarande added, "You're supposed to be resting." The idea of disappearing and reappearing someplace else did not make him comfortable. The fae probably did it all the time, but he would prefer not being at their mercy. Again.

"When they said resting, they meant no magic use," Reaghan explained. "It drains more energy than physical exertion."

"I could always conjure something for the two of you to ride in," Pwyll offered.

"I think that would be a better solution," Amarande readily

175

accepted.

Reaghan nodded. "I agree."

Pwyll snapped his fingers and a two-man carriage appeared.

Amarande frowned. "How do you steer it?"

Pwyll chuckled. "You don't. At least not like a human machine." He gestured to the carriage. "It will take you where you want to go. You just need to think about your destination and it will route you there."

"It's not going to run over innocent by-standers along the way, is it?" Amarande asked.

"No." Pwyll's grin widened. "It's magic, as you humans say. Just trust that it will work without injury to you or anyone around you."

Reaghan tugged on Amarande's hand. "Come. I'll show you."

He somewhat reluctantly helped her into the seat then climbed in next to her.

"Thank you, Pwyll." Reaghan smiled at her brother.

"Take care." He looked at Amarande. "Both of you."

Reaghan waved as the carriage rolled forward then reached for Amarande's hand.

There was a lot they needed to settle in a very short time and he wasn't sure how it would go. Fear that he might still lose her churned in his gut.

Reaghan pointed out buildings and artwork as they passed. Despite his best efforts, he couldn't help but notice the double-takes and open stares they received from the people they passed. Obviously they were not used to seeing vampires in their city.

Relief swamped him when they finally stopped. When he climbed off the carriage and helped her down, a ray of light filtered through the overhanging tree limbs and illuminated the welt on his arm. "Is the sun different here than in the human realm?" He asked as they walked the twisting pathway to the door. "I'm surprised my skin has not blistered."

"Oh!" Reaghan pulled his hand up so she could inspect it. "With all the craziness, that never occurred to me. I'll have to ask Caoilfhinn next time I see her." She gestured at the door of what appeared to be a bungalow type home.

"Does Pwyll leave his door unlocked all the time?" Amarande asked.

"Hhmmm?" She looked back to where he inspected the door. "No." She smiled. "We don't need doors with latches and locks like humans. Everything is protected with charms. Pwyll encoded his home to only allow certain people entrance. He would have pushed energy into the coding, if you will, of the charms to allow you and I to pass through the barrier. The door is mostly an illusion that grants privacy."

"Interesting," Amarande closed the door then followed her into the sitting room.

Like most bachelors, Pwyll's tastes were fairly simple. There wasn't a lot of furniture or decorations. Neutral shades of brown covered most of the furniture and floors, while blues and green broke up the drabness in the cushions and accessories. The space actually had a little bit of an un-lived-in feel. Almost like a luxury hotel.

"Do you need refreshment?" she asked.

His gaze was instantly drawn to her neck. "A really big glass of water sounds fabulous."

She headed for the back of the space but he grabbed her hand to stop her. "You are supposed to rest. Just point me in the right direction and I'll get some for both of us."

"I'm not sure you'd understand how things work here so how about if we do it together?" She offered. "Then next time you'll know."

She showed him how to work the fresh water flow and together they piled fruits and berries into a bowl. With their hands full of refreshments, they went to the den.

She took a seat next to him but left far more distance between them than he cared for. He pulled her right up next to him.

She looked up at him and asked, "Why did you do it? Why did you take the chance and enter our realm?"

"Because you might have died if I didn't."

"You had to know you could have been killed as soon as you crossed through the portal."

He shrugged. "Who wants to live forever anyway?"

"I do." She intertwined her fingers with his and added, "As long as you're with me."

The weight on his chest lightened, but he had to ask. "Are you certain of what you're saying? Because from what I've seen, vampires are not highly regarded around here. Your family and friends may not be very supportive."

"I know."

He waited for her to continue, but she didn't. "And you'd be fine knowing that?"

"The alternative is living without you. And that really isn't much of an option."

He pulled her into his lap and leaned her back on the seat. "You have no idea how glad I am to hear that." He kissed her with every ounce of passion he possessed. It was vital that he show her how much she meant to him. The words might not be there, but the feelings were.

When he finally pulled back, he looked deep into her eyes. "When I found you in your hotel room, and I thought I had lost you. I wanted to die right alongside of you."

She touched his face as tears rolled down her cheeks. "But I didn't die."

He pressed a kiss against the inside of her wrist. "I know. And I thank God for it."

"What about your own family? Your clan."

"Edrigu and Shaia will both understand." He shrugged. "It might take a while for some of the other lords to accept you but that is their problem. Not mine."

"But—" She tried to sit up, but his weight leaning over her stopped her. "I thought you said you had hoped to become a Clan Leader one day?"

"I did hope to someday."

"But won't your attachment to me get in the way? Even if we were to go to the human realm?"

"I don't see going back to the human realm as much of an option."

"Why not?"

"Because I heard what you told Eirin. That your powers will fade and you will lose your memory of being fae. I don't want you to have to give up everything and die a mortal's death just so I can stay in the human realm. I'd rather have a nice long life with you right here."

"It's true that when a fae breaks ties with Eolande, they lose what makes them fae. We get our power and our strength from our families and this realm. Is there a reason that we can't live in both places?"

"You mean travel back and forth between realms?" He wanted to make sure of what she was suggesting.

"Yes."

"Would your king and queen mind if we did that?"

"We won't know unless we ask them."

"I just want you. Whether we stay here in Eolande or go back to the human realm. As long as you are in my life I will figure out the rest."

She wrapped her arms around him tightly and kissed him. When he finally pulled back they were both grinning like fools.

"Has there ever been a vampire-fae marriage?" he asked.

Reaghan shook her head. "None that were acknowledged or accepted by the fae. At least, not in my lifetime. Of course, there are always rumors of fae disappearing into the human realm. Some were reportedly taken and eaten by a vampire. Others were sensational tales of reckless love."

A wicked grin spread across his face. He leaned closer and nuzzled the side of her neck. "I would wager that you wouldn't mind if I ate you."

A wave of warmth washed over her as she melted against him. "No." She whispered. "I probably wouldn't mind at all."

He chuckled as he gave her a quick nibble on her ear.

"So what do you say? Shall we be trendsetters and show the stodgy old guard just how well vampires and fae can get along?"

She grinned. "Perhaps not in vivid detail. But yes, I do believe we could set an example of how glorious life can be when you follow your heart."

"Then shall we get started, my love?"

Her grin grew wider as she wrapped her arms around his neck. "Indeed."

EPILOGUE

CALLUM dropped his hammer in the bucket with a thud. The scrap pieces of wood he had cut off went in next. As he finished folding the ladder he had been using his spine stiffened.

Without turning around he knew he was no longer alone.

"What do you want?" Callum groused.

"That's no way to greet your favorite brother."

"According to *your* mother, I don't have a brother. I am a bastard reject with no family at all."

Lairgnen grimaced. "You and I both know the queen could be an un-feeling bitch. She made father pay dearly for daring to fall in love with your mother. Knowing that he had a half-human child somewhere in the human realm bothered her more than all of his infidelities."

Callum turned and shot a glare at Lairgnen. "Don't you have Fae King business to tend to?"

"Of course I do. Why do you think I'm here?"

"To annoy me."

Lairgnen chuckled. "That's merely a bonus." He conjured a small chair and took a seat.

Callum continued cleaning up his tools and things as if Lairgnen's presence didn't matter.

Because it didn't.

Not really.

"Why did you tell the vampire where the portal was?" Lairgnen finally asked.

Callum scoffed. "Because he asked nicely."

"Seriously." Lairgnen leaned forward and rested his royal elbows on his knees. "Why?"

Even though Callum actively searched for signs of deceit all he found was sincerity in Lairgnen's eyes. "Because I could tell that she mattered to him. Deeply. I also knew how close she was to dying. Going home was her best shot at surviving."

"Some say you failed in your duty."

Callum glared at Lairgnen. "Some might be idiots."

"True. But you did allow a mortal to pass through the portal."

"Amarande is vampire. He isn't mortal."

Lairgnen's lip twitched in a semblance of a smile. "Valid point." Then his expression turned serious again. "You know she lived, don't you?"

Callum nodded. "They hunted me down when they returned from Eolande." He wiped the sawdust off of the window ledge below where he had been working. "I guess they thought they needed to thank me."

"Is that hard for you?"

"What's that?" Callum looked up from his task.

"Accepting gratitude."

Callum shrugged.

"I understand you arranged for them to meet with Doran Kavanaugh."

How did Lairgnen know that? Even if he was king of the fae, why did he care what happened in the human realm? "Doran is the Pack Alpha for this area. He was the one I turned the shifters who attacked Amarande and Reaghan over to. As it turns out, they were rogue. Doran wanted Amarande and Reaghan's testimony before deciding punishment."

"I assume they came to some agreement that satisfied Amarande's need for vengeance and Doran's need for pack solidarity?"

"Of course."

"And he figured out who hired the shifters, correct?"

Callum gave Lairgnen a hard look. "Why do you even bother asking me if you already know?"

Lairgnen chuckled.

Callum shook his head and went back to what he was doing. If he ignored his half-brother he would eventually leave. His family never wanted anything to do with him in the past. He doubted it would be any different now that Lairgnen had become king.

"I envy what you have here."

"What? This castle?" Callum scoffed. "This isn't mine. I'm merely one of many caretakers here. And I feel certain that whatever you live in is far grander than what I do live in."

"I meant your life. Your freedom."

"You're free to go where ever you want," Callum pointed out. "And you obviously have the power to do so. With or without portals."

"That is only partially true. The responsibility for an entire race, one that is slowly dying out and often fights itself, weighs heavy. I am not as free as you might think."

He faced his brother. "Then why did you fight for the crown. You could have easily passed it up."

Lairgnen grimaced. "Not really. If I had not stepped up to accept the challenge, we would have had to wait more than two decades in human years until the next in line would have been of age to even accept the challenge. If she failed the challenge, we might have been without a king or queen for a hundred years." A pained expression crossed his face. "Do you know what our council is like?"

"Thankfully, no."

"They're spoiled children who bicker damn near constantly."

Callum smirked. "Spoiled children with the ability to turn you into a dust bunny?"

That got a chuckle from Lairgnen. "Yes."

"Job has to have some perks."

"So far the only perk is the sword."

Ah, yes. The infamous sword of Finvarra. It was rumored to give the one chosen to carry it the power to defeat any enemy. Even from what little Callum knew of fae customs, that was how the fae king was selected.

"What about your wife?" Callum asked.

"I would have her with or without the job. And just so you know, she's the only thing keeping me sane."

The faint stirrings of jealousy took Callum by surprise. Just because he was alone didn't mean everyone else had to be. "It's good you have her then."

"Your time is coming, you know." Lairgnen conjured a portal with the snap of his fingers. "You cannot run from destiny. Or love. In the end, it rules us all." He smiled and stepped through the gateway.

"I guess we'll see."

"The offer I made you after Father's passing remains. You're welcome in Eolande anytime you wish."

"Yeah, I heard you the first time."

"I'll keep reminding you." With one last nod Lairgnen returned to the fae realm.

Callum sank onto the nearby bench and rubbed his head.

He knew his time was coming. He sensed it. The very air around him felt different as if all of the elements were lining up to take a shot at him.

Why, though?

There is nothing remarkable about me.

Lairgnen's laugh echoed in Callum's head. *Ah…but there is something remarkable about your union with Her.*

The End

If you enjoyed this book, please consider leaving a review!

ABOUT THE AUTHOR

Dena Garson is an award-winning author of contemporary, paranormal, fantasy, and sci-fi romance. She holds a BBA and a MBA in Business and works in the wacky world of quality and process improvement. Making up her own reality on paper is what keeps her sane.

She is the mother of two rowdy boys and two rambunctious cats (AKA the fuzzy jerks). When she isn't writing you can find her at the sewing machine or stringing beads. She is also a devoted Whovian and Dallas Cowboys fan.

Find Dena on the web at:

Website - http://www.denagarson.com/
Facebook- https://www.facebook.com/AuthorDenaGarson
Twitter - https://twitter.com/DenaGarson
Email – Dena@DenaGarson.com

OTHER BOOKS BY DENA GARSON

Steampunk
Christmas Royale
Her Clockwork Heart
To London, With Love

Paranormal/Fantasy/Sci-Fi Romance
Ghostly Persuasion
Mystic's Touch
Rege's Rescue
Vordol's Vow
When Ash Remains
Your Wild Heart

Contemporary Romance
Down to Business
Loss of Control
Risky Business
Snow Effect

Find detailed information on all of Dena's books at:
http://www.denagarson.com/books.html

OTHER EMERALD ISLE ENCHANTMENT BOOKS

Tell Me Your Secrets by Virginia Cavanaugh

Ghostly Persuasion by Dena Garson

Phantom Mischief by J.L. LaRose

Lord Griffin's Prize by Katalina Leon

An Irish Flirtation by Louisa Masters
An Irish Attraction by Louisa Masters

Crimson Lust by Rebecca Royce

Desire and the Djinn by Rea Thomas

# EXCERPT
From *Ghostly Persuasion*

"OH my God, Jenny. You should see this place," Katie exclaimed into the phone.

"Is it as wonderful as their website showed?"

"Even better." Katie spun herself around in the middle of her suite. The furnishings and the ambience and the fact that she was in a twelfth- century castle still held her in awe. "They must have done a lot of work to keep this place in such good shape."

"I'll bet. You do have indoor plumbing then, huh?" Jenny teased.

"It looks like I have my own spa in here," Katie said as she paraded back into the marble-lined bathroom for the fifth time. "The bathtub could hold three of me and the shower has one of those fancy waterfall fixtures. Funny thing is, despite it being completely covered with stone or tile, it's not cold. I think the floor is heated somehow."

"Oooo… Send me a picture so I can be even more jealous."

"I hate it that Mom spent so much money. There is no way this was a cheap trip."

"Your mom loved you, Katie. Just think of it as her way of spoiling you one last time."

Katie sighed into the phone. "I really miss her."

"I know you do. So do I."

Katie sniffed back the tears she felt coming and forced herself to focus on how wonderful her room was. "All right, I better go. I need to see if I can get some sleep so I can adjust to this time zone. And I don't want to run up a huge phone bill."

"Okay. I'm glad you made it safely." Jenny yawned, making Katie regret waking her up so early.

"I'll let you know what I'm doing throughout the week."

"Okay, sis. You have fun over there. And keep an eye out for available, hunky Irishmen."

Katie rolled her eyes. "Yeah, okay. I'll be sure I do that."

"Send me pictures when you do," Jenny said with another yawn.

"Uh huh. Sorry to wake you. I'll talk to you later."

Katie clicked off her cell phone and dropped it into her jeans pocket. She unpacked about half of her clothes as she dug around looking for clean underwear and a t-shirt to sleep in. Her body felt tired but she wasn't sleepy and the lure of the oversized bathtub was more than she could resist.

She turned on the water, found a temperature to suit her then added some of the bath salts that were sitting on the ledge over the tub. The smell of fresh lavender floated up with the steam rising from the water.

If that didn't help her relax, nothing would.

She dropped her dirty clothes onto the floor then kicked them into the corner, out of the way. She made a mental note to find her laundry bag later. Just before stepping into the decadent-smelling water and steam, she remembered to grab an extra towel off the rack at the end of the counter.

When she sank into the steamy bath she sighed with pleasure.

Now this she could get used to quickly.

Katie allowed her thoughts to drift and float where they wanted. Some of them were based in reality, like what she would need to do about finding a roommate when she returned home. The others were nowhere near being real. Her mind strayed to the idea that a hunky Irishman showed up in her room and offered to rub away all her aches and pains. He, of course, would know exactly where to touch her and would want nothing more than to spend all day and night pleasuring her.

Then, after making love to her multiple times, he would declare his undying devotion to her.

She snorted to herself. Yeah right. And maybe monkeys will fly out of my butt too.

It was a lovely daydream however. Especially the part where she had three orgasms before leaving the bathroom. Twice in the tub and once while bent over the vanity counter. Her fantasy man was extremely talented.

Katie sighed as she stepped out of the tub. It was too bad no such man existed outside of Jenny's beloved romance novels.

As she dried off she thought about her last few boyfriends. None of them had created that special spark she felt should have been there. As much as she cared for her last boyfriend Alan, she was glad now that he had panicked and broken up with her right before their college graduation. It hurt at the time but, looking back, it had been the right thing.

She hadn't told Alan about her "gift". That alone should have been a big indicator the relationship wasn't going to work. If she didn't feel comfortable enough confiding that information, something had definitely been missing.

After rubbing some lotion on, she slipped into a clean pair of boyshorts and pulled a t-shirt over her head. With her hair wrapped in a towel, she padded out to the bedroom. As soon as she had a clear view of the four-poster bed she skidded to a stop, stunned by the sight of a strange man lounging against the headboard.

"Excuse me, but what are you doing?" Katie demanded.

The man continued to stare up at the ceiling with his hands behind his head as if he hadn't heard her. He appeared to be deep in thought.

Katie was distracted from her irritation by the sight of his wide shoulders. Her mouth went dry as she ogled the stranger. Even through the linen shirt she could see he did more than computer programming or living a life of luxury. He had a rugged look to him that said he knew how to work with his hands and his body. Her eyes were drawn to the patch of bare skin exposed by the open V of his shirt then down to the waistband of his trousers. His tan pants looked as if they were part of a period costume but fit his long, muscular legs nicely.

The way he lounged on her bed with his legs spread across the coverlet made her think that he had no plans to leave anytime soon.

She mentally shook herself back to the situation. There was a man, although a very masculine and, well, let's face it, a downright yummy man, in her room. She didn't know him and she certainly hadn't invited him in.

"Uh, hello?" she said a little louder, trying to position herself behind the nearest chair, hoping to hide the fact that she wore very few clothes.

The man didn't even twitch.

"Hey! You there." Katie watched the man closely, looking for any kind of response but only saw a slight twitch in one foot. "Can you hear me?"

Either the man was deaf or he had earphones in. His reddish-blond hair had been tied back, giving her a clear view of one ear. There were no cords hanging down. Perhaps he had a wireless device? She hated to draw attention to herself given her lack of clothing but didn't believe she had another option since she had left her cell phone on the bedside table right next to the hotel phone.

She checked the area around her for something to toss onto the bed. If she could get the man's attention she'd simply point out he had entered the wrong room and he needed to leave. There were a few breakable trinkets on the bookshelf behind her along with, obviously, books. She spotted a small metal dish within reach. Since she wasn't sure how valuable any of the items were, she opted for the item least likely to break.

The bed was only fifteen or twenty feet away. Surely she could Frisbee the dish onto the bed? Maybe even make it land right next to the man. That should be enough to get his notice.

"Hey, Mr. Hunky Irishman! You need to get out of my room!" Katie said in a much louder voice. Still no response.

Okay. Katie stepped to the side of the tall-backed chair so she could leverage the dish properly. Here goes nothing.

The tarnished silver dish sailed across the span and landed on the foot of the bed as she planned. Thanks to the flat, smooth bottom, the dish skimmed across the bedspread and into the man lying on the bed.

Into the man. She blinked mutely.

Not up next to him.

Not bounced off.

Into the man.

Katie gaped at him, unsure of what she had seen. He looked real. He appeared to be corporeal. He didn't have the hazy, semi-transparent body that she associated with most spirits. But the dish had passed through him.

What the hell was he then?

As she stared, he turned his head and looked at her. Their eyes met. Katie's chest ached at the loneliness she saw in the depths of his gaze. Before she realized what she was doing she had stepped around the chair and moved toward him.

He sat up suddenly and asked, "You can see me, can't you?"

His native accent lent even more appeal to his deep, baritone voice. Even though she heard the faint echoey sound she associated with spirits, she had a very physical reaction. This was one of those rare men she would gladly listen to as he read stereo instructions.

Katie gave a slight, hesitant nod. She didn't like revealing her gift but figured her face and her reactions had already given her away.

The man jumped up and crossed the room quicker than she'd anticipated. With a squeak of alarm she darted behind the chair when he came to stand right in front of her.

"Who are you? And what are you doing in my room?" she demanded, pulling her courage around her like a cloak.

"Ah, lass, you have nothing to fear from me." He spread his hands out in front of him in a placating manner.

"I'll be the judge of that, thank you very much."

He tipped his head. "I apologize for startling you. It's been a good many years since someone other than the local specters could see or hear me. My excitement got the better of me."

"Yeah, well..." Katie stammered. "I can kinda understand that." She tucked a strand of hair behind her ear. "So, who are you?"

"Seamus MacDonhnaill." He made a short bow. "Formerly of the County Donegal MacDonhnaills."

"Formerly? Does that mean you got kicked out of that county or that family?"

He chuckled. The deep, rich sound sent ripples of warmth down to her core.

"Neither, actually." He cocked his head to one side and regarded her. "I have simply considered myself a resident of Tullamore Castle for some time now."

"Ah." The way he said resident make Katie think he did more than live here. She cleared her throat nervously. "I, uh... I don't want to be rude or anything, but I'm not comfortable standing here talking with someone I don't know when I'm only half- dressed."

Seamus' eyes quickly glanced down at the chair she had been using to keeping her modesty in place.

"Would you mind stepping out for a moment while I dig out a pair of jeans or something?" Katie asked. Seamus raised an eyebrow in question but Katie rushed on, "I know it's silly with you being..." Words failed her. Was Seamus a ghost? If so, he was unlike any she had come across before. "Uh, not quite solid, but I have a rule about being fully dressed when I meet new people."

Katie forced a smile on her face, even though she knew she had turned bright-pink from embarrassment.

To his credit, Seamus didn't laugh but he did a poor job of hiding his smirk. "Very well. When you're comfortable, simply open your door." Seamus moved to the door then paused and turned to look at her. With a mischievous grin he added, "I look forward to meeting you properly."

Katie frowned at Seamus' back as he passed through the closed door and disappeared from her sight.

She scampered to her suitcase and pulled out a clean pair of jeans. As she zipped them up it occurred to her that while she had demanded to know Seamus' name, she hadn't given him hers.

That had been very rude! Mom would have been appalled.

Shaking her head in disgust over her lack of manners, Katie dug in the pocket on the lid of her suitcase for a bra. She looked over her shoulder to where she's last seen Seamus, just to make sure he hadn't floated back in. Reassured that she still had the room to herself, Katie unwound the towel from around her hair and head then quickly pulled her shirt up and put her bra on.

Part of her wondered why she even bothered. After all, as a spirit, Seamus wouldn't be able to do anything other than look. A flash of warmth zipped down her spine at the thought that he would look.

Too bad he wasn't flesh and bone. She'd actually consider taking Jenny's advice if Seamus was the "hunky Irishman".

Now that she was fully dressed she felt less exposed. She went into the bathroom, grabbed her brush then she sat on the edge of the bed and debated the wisdom of inviting Seamus back in as she brushed the tangles from her hair. Yes, he knew she could see him but didn't know the extent of her gift. If he had an ounce of sense he'd ask, however. And right now, she didn't know what she'd tell him.

Why did Seamus appear different than other ghosts she had encountered? If that dish hadn't passed through him she wouldn't have realized he was a spirit. She needed to find out what he really was.

A picture of Seamus' face when he first looked at her popped into her mind's eye. In those brief seconds she had seen a loneliness so deep it created a knot in her chest when she recalled it. Had he really not talked with anyone other than a few ghosts in a long time?

She couldn't turn him away.

Besides, it wasn't as if he were pox-ridden with weeping sores or anything else disgusting. As a matter of fact, she found him a little too easy to look at.

Katie took a deep breath and released it. Her mind made up, she went to the door and swung it open. Disappointment rippled through her when she didn't find him waiting there.

She stepped out into the hallway and looked in both directions. The only thing she saw was a full set of armor standing guard a little ways down the hall, across from her room.

"Seamus?" Katie called quietly. She didn't hear a response or spot him anywhere. Where would he have gone? She shrugged and stepped back into her room, leaving the door ajar to let Seamus know he could come in if he returned.

With her head down, she didn't notice Seamus standing in the middle of the room until she practically ran into him.

"Jesus!" She jumped back in alarm. "Don't do that!"

"Do what?" Seamus asked even though a smiled played across his lips.

"Just… Just…" Katie shook her open hand in his direction to indicate she meant all of him. "Just show up like that. Can't you knock or something?"

"Actually—"

"Oh, never mind," she said, exasperated. Her heart raced from the startle and she struggled to get it under control. "I know you can't knock but you should announce yourself instead of just poofing in. Sheesh."

"Poofing? I don't think I have ever poofed in to anything." Seamus sounded somewhat insulted.

"Oh you know what I mean." Katie stomped over to the couch. "One minute you're not there and suddenly you are." She dropped onto her chosen seat then waved in Seamus' direction. "Poof."

"Ah. I see." He followed her to the sitting area and took a seat at the other end of the couch. "I'm guessing that I don't always manifest this state in a way that you can see me."

"This state?"

"Before I answer your obvious question, I believe that you owe me an introduction."

"Oh my God." Katie sat up straight on the couch. "I'm so sorry. I'm normally not that rude. My name is Katherine, well, Katie, to my friends, Ward. From America."

193

"Katherine Ward." Seamus smiled. "I had deduced by your accent that you are from the Americas. What brings you to Tullamore?"

Katie pulled her feet up under her. "I'm bringing my mother's ashes home."

Seamus dipped his head. "I'm sorry for your loss. Did she recently pass?"

"No. Actually she died about three years ago." At the questioning look in his eye she added, "I wasn't told of her request to be brought home to Ireland until a couple of weeks ago."

"Then I'm doubly sorry for your loss." He regarded her for a moment. "Your mother was Irish then." It was a statement more than a question.

"Yes."

"You do look like a daughter of Ireland." A frown creased his forehead as he continued to study her.

Katie squirmed nervously. "Did I suddenly sprout horns out of the top of my head?" she finally asked, uncomfortable with the way Seamus looked at her.

"You look like someone I've seen before." He absently rubbed his chin as he got lost in his thoughts once again. Then he shook his head as if to clear it and said, "I'll think of it later."

"If you say so," Katie mumbled. "So," she said brightly, changing the subject. "How did you come to be a spirit at Tullamore? Were you mortally wounded in battle on the castle grounds? Or did you fall off one of the castle walls during a siege? Or anything like that?"

Seamus' face darkened. Katie instinctively leaned back, away from the rage and disgust she saw in his eyes.

"I was cursed by a whore pretending to be a lady."